Percy St.-John
and
The Chronicle of Secrets

E.A. Allen

Percy St.-John and The Chronicle of Secrets

Histria Kids

Las Vegas ◊ Oxford ◊ Palm Beach

Published in the United States of America by Histria Books,
a division of Histria LLC
7181 N. Hualapai Way, Ste. 130-86
Las Vegas, NV 89166 USA
HistriaBooks.com

Histria Kids is an imprint of Histria Books. Titles published under the imprints of Histria Books are distributed worldwide.

Library of Congress Control Number: 2020950997

ISBN 978-1-59211-084-1 (hardcover)

Contents

Dedication

For Divinika, Jennifer, Patrick, Samuel, Tabitha, and Zoe —
The Young Readers Gang at the Fayetteville Public Library.
Your thoughtful insights and critiques made Percy a much
better yarn. My profound thanks.

I could a tale unfold, Whose lightest word would harrow up thy soul...

— Hamlet

Editor's Notes*

What is a monastery?

A monastery is a building where some men have formed a religious community, to devote themselves to prayer and thinking about God. These men are called monks, and they usually take a vow to devote their lives to prayer and work. Monasteries are a tradition of the Catholic Church and date back to about the year 550. The rules that govern such communities are very strict and require monks to pray often throughout the day, work hard, and remain silent for long periods. Monks often chant their prayers. The head of the monastery is called an Abbot. Monasteries are often located in remote places, far away from the temptations of the outside world. Other religions, such as Buddhism and Taoism, also have monasteries.

The Monastic Day (Hours)* The monastic day is highly scheduled and segmented into times of prayer, called Hours. Between Hours, monks eat, sleep, and work. The Hours of the Monastic Day have varied over the centuries and even somewhat between monasteries.

Matins (2:30-3:00 a.m.)
Lauds (5:00-6:00 a.m.)
Prime (7:30 a.m.)
Terce (9:00 a.m.)
Sext (noon)
Nones (2:00-3:00 p.m.)
Vespers (4:30 p.m.)
Compline (6:00 p.m.)

*For the meaning of other unusual terms see the Glossary at the end of the story.

Prologue
Wherein Percy's Life Changes Forever

A Road, near Brixly, in Surrey
November 1906

1

"Good Heavens, it's cold!" he groused to himself, pulling up the collar of his coat 'round his ears. He walked briskly along the lonely road, an icy night wind biting his face. The duties of a village vicar are often painful, he muttered. He'd just been to the widow Colby's house, comforting the old woman in her serious illness. God bless her, he mused, the poor old thing's not likely to endure much longer.

As he walked the road narrowed to a wagon rut passing through thick shrubs and trees to either side. Looking down and breasting the wind, the vicar stopped short, aware of something in front of him. It was the form of a large man, his arms akimbo, standing astride the path.

"Oh, it's you vicar," the man said, in a rough voice. "'ad no thought to see you out on a night such as this. A raw one, eh?"

The vicar did not recognize the shape in front of him — not his face, which was obscured by darkness, nor his voice, which somehow seemed menacing.

"A raw night, indeed, my friend. So, I'll bid you a good evening and be on my way."

As the vicar stepped forward, however, the large man moved to block his progress.

"What is it?" asked the vicar.

"'Tis a matter of help for the poor, vicar."

"A worthy thing, my friend, but perhaps you could come see me at the vicarage, in the morning...?

"I'll be makin' m'request just now if you please vicar. The situation is urgent, you see, and there's no time to wait."

Just then the vicar heard a noise from behind him, and as he turned felt a heavy thud at the back of his head. It was the last sensation of his life, for just then another blow from the front smashed his forehead. Uttering only a faint gasp, he fell to the road in a heap, and the men fell upon him, searching his pockets. Then one stood, once again placing his hands on his hips.

"Damnation! There ain't nothin' 'ere. The blighter's pockets are empty."

The other thief rose, holding a small book in his hands. "Only this. A bloody book of prayers. Ain't worth nothin' for sure. But 'is coat must be worth somethin'. And 'is shoes."

As the two began to tear at the vicar's clothes the big thug noticed the glint of something in the moonlight. Reaching down, he tore it from the dead vicar's chest.

"What 'er it?" the other asked eagerly, leaning in.

Holding the object up to the light, the big man replied. "A cross. Looks t' be gold, maybe. And, set with some stones too." He smiled. "Maybe we'll be rewarded for our good night's work, eh?"

The two turned and vanished into the hedges. A sudden burst of the wind howled through the leafless trees.

"What is it!" said Percy, as he sat bolt upright in his bed. It was banging at the front door, and then the muffled sound of frantic voices. He could make out the familiar voice of Mrs. Warren, the vicarage housekeeper. But not the voices of the men.

Then, the door to his bedchamber flew open. "Who? What?" he asked, rubbing his eyes as the bright light of lamps startled him.

"Help him dress, Mrs. Warren," one of the men ordered in a rough voice. "Father? Where's father," Percy begged, as the woman took one arm and the men retreated to the outer room. The housekeeper said nothing as she handed Percy his clothes, but he could hear her sobbing. "Why, Mrs. Warren? Why are you crying?" No answer, as she helped him with his shirt.

When the two emerged from the bedchamber into the foyer of the vicarage, Percy could see three men, all of them wearing tall hats and stern faces. They were all men of the Parish Council and the oldest he knew to be Mr. Stanton, the village solicitor. At first, Mr. Stanton hesitated, but then he spoke.

"There's been a... there's been a tragedy, Percy... er... about your father, the vicar."

"A tragedy?" the boy repeated. "Where's father?" he gasped, looking around.

The men looked at each other as if deciding who was going to say it.

"About your father, boy. He's dead."

The wind suddenly went out of Percy, as if his lungs had collapsed. Then he gasped and turned to Mrs. Warren. "Is it true?" he pleaded, now crying right along with the housekeeper.

"Yes," she said in a low voice, choking back more tears. "Yes, Percy. 'Tis."

The old housekeeper took Percy in her arms to comfort him, as the visitors turned and left, closing the door behind them.

Percy passed the rest of the night in alternating spells of tears and numb disbelief. Mrs. Warren wept along with him. Finally, he began to ask the questions — "Where? How did it happen? Who?"

At first, Mrs. Warren hesitated to tell him what she'd heard, or to say anything at all, fearing the details would only make things worse. But Percy persisted and insisted on knowing.

"Murdered," she explained. "Almost certainly by thieves, as he came 'long the road from the widow Colby's house. He'd nothing of value on him — not even his coin-purse — when they found him, so it was robbery the foul demons were after," she explained, shaking her head.

Hearing the details Percy fell back once more into tears.

2

Next day, some of the women of the parish came to pay their respects. Mrs. Warren insisted that Percy must put on his Sunday suit and receive them in the proper way. Most brought food and stayed just long enough to say how sad they were at the vicar's death, and what a fine man he was, and he would surely be missed by everyone.

In the evening, Percy learned the Parish Council and Vicar Panford, from a nearby village, had decided to have the funeral and burial the next day. They had also decided that no one was to see the Vicar's body, not even Percy, "owing," it was said, "to the condition of things." When Percy asked, Mrs. Warren explained that meant his father's head and face were "not to be looked upon."

The passing hours became mainly a daze to Percy. He wept often until he could cry no more, and then he closed his eyes and thought about his father and told himself often that he must reconcile that he was gone and not to return. He'd gone to Heaven, as he so often said he wished to do, and so it was not such a terrible thing. And then he told himself that it was a terrible thing, and why had God allowed such a fine man to be murdered and left on the road? Sometimes Percy told himself that it was not real and that his father, somehow, would return and show everyone that it had been a mistake. Someone else had been killed, but not him. He was alive and well and on his way home. And then he did not come.

Next day, Mrs. Warren led Percy by the hand through all the rituals of the funeral. Standing and then sitting beside the wooden box, which Percy knew contained the body of his father, he did not hear all that was said, because he was thinking to himself that it was, after all, his good-bye to his father. The last he would be with him — close to him, even if he was in the dreaded box.

The procession to the churchyard and the open grave was brief, and then, with prayers, the men of the parish lowered the box into the ground and began to cover it with dirt. Percy stood watching, sometimes crying and sometimes not, but watching everything that was part of his father's going — listening to the awful hollow thud of every shovel of dirt as it hit the top of the box. When the covering was done, everyone left the churchyard. Percy and Mrs. Warren remained standing beside the grave, looking at the mound of dirt and the rough wooden cross that would mark the spot until a proper stone could be made. It was only then that Percy felt completely alone.

3

Percy's dazed awareness of his father's death soon gave way to anger. Anger at being left alone. Anger at those who'd murdered his father and would likely escape their proper punishment. Anger at everyone who now seemed to have forgotten him. And yes, even anger at God for having allowed his father — the finest and best man in the world — to be murdered in such a way. And then, just anger about everything. About life itself. Until anger became a comfort of sorts.

After several days, during which Percy mostly sat brooding in his father's study and wandering aimlessly about the vicarage, brooding turned to wondering what would become of him. Where would he go? What could he do? Who would be his family?

Those questions were answered more quickly than Percy expected. Three days after the funeral, Mr. Stanton and several of the Parish Council came to the vicarage and invited Percy to join them in the study.

"Yes?" Percy said, not knowing what the visitors were about nor what was to come next.

"Well, there's a development, Master Percy, that concerns you. Yes, concerns you very definitely," said Mr. Stanton.

Percy didn't like the cold look in Mr. Stanton's eyes or the somber tone of his voice. The others looked down.

"A development? What's that?" he asked, not knowing what to expect, but sensing that only a painful answer could come from his question.

"We've had a reply to our cable to your grandfather. The Vicar's father, eh? And he...

Mr. Stanton paused in mid-sentence and drew a breath.

"Though he acknowledges, as he must in law, that you are his heir, he says bluntly he'll have nothing to do with you and particularly he takes no responsibility for you."

Percy closed his eyes and swallowed hard, uncertain what all that meant. He'd never met his grandfather and his father had told him long ago that the old man wished to have nothing to do with them, though he could not disown them entirely.

"But, what's to become of me then?" Percy finally asked.

"Your grandfather has made some modest provision, knowing that he must, for you to be taken to an institution near London. He has given the County Council a sum of money for your upkeep while you are in the... eh...

"...while I am in the orphanage! You are sending me to an orphanage!" Percy shouted in disbelief.

"There's nothing to be done, boy," said Mr. Stanton, sternly. "And so that's the end of it. Mrs. Warren will have you ready to travel in the morning."

And with that, the men departed, leaving Percy alone. Mrs. Warren had gone to her sister's for the evening, Percy knew, and would not be back till morning.

In the eerie quiet of the vicarage and with time to consider, Percy grasped the full seriousness of what was about to happen to him. That he'd been abandoned by everyone. And that he had no means to survive except by his own resources. It was the sense of being so completely alone that now caused him to fall to tears. That and once again grieving the loss of his father.

Percy lay crying on his bed until he lost consciousness and went to sleep. He awakened some hours later, at first light. It was then he realized that for some reason Mrs. Warren had not returned, as she should have by that time. The vicarage was still empty.

Percy's emotions now gave way to a sense of panic. Even Mrs. Warren, it seemed, had abandoned him. All he could think was that he was about to be taken to the orphanage and he desperately did not want to go there. A place that to him was like a prison.

Sensing that time was short, he scrambled under his bed for the carpetbag his father had sometimes used. He began to fill it with his belongings. He ran to his father's study, wondering what things of his father's he should take to remember him. He couldn't think clearly or take time to consider, so he just began to take things at random from the desk. A pen. A note pad. A journal. He crammed them all into the bag.

Next, he ran to the kitchen, thinking he would need food for the road. He was now determined to run away as quickly as he could. Anything to avoid the terrible fate of the orphanage. In the kitchen, he found a tin of hard biscuits and a piece of cheese, and tossed them both into the bag.

Now he was ready to make his escape. 'Should I go out the door?' he wondered. 'No. It'll be watched. The window. My bedchamber window is the way to go,' he reasoned. 'A window that will put me on the path through the woods and past the village without being seen.'

Opening the sash, he tossed his bag out first and then climbed after it. As soon as his feet touched the ground, however, he felt the grip of a cold hand on his neck. A strong and unforgiving hand.

"Mr. Stanton said you might try this," said a scolding voice. Percy looked behind him and could see it was Constable Meeks, the local policeman.

Percy began to kick and scream, trying with all his might to shake free of the hand on his neck. He flailed about, as he was being dragged around the corner of the vicarage and onto the high street.

There, he could see a coach waiting, with Mr. Stanton standing beside the open door.

"In here, Master Percy," Mr. Stanton said, with no particular emotion.

Percy screamed that he refused to go and again attempted to free himself from the constable, but to no avail. Meeks forced him into the coach and came in after him, never releasing his neck.

"Whip-up, driver," Meeks ordered.

As the coach passed along the village high street, Percy sobbed and looked out the window, knowing he would never see his home again.

Chapter One

Wherein I Begin to See People
Who Are Not There

Five Years Later. The Benedictine Monastery of St. Ambrose,
Near Chaumont, Switzerland
April 1911

1

I don't remember much about it myself. That day, I mean. I recall the icy cold and the sleet against my face. I remember the crying woman in the red scarf — the one who kissed me and said "I love you" and then disappeared across the stone bridge and down the road.

I believe I am fourteen, though I'm not sure. The brother monks say I've been here ten years — here in our monastery of Saint Ambrose — and they reckon I was four years old that day I was left at their gate. They say I didn't know my name, so they called me Gabriel. You know, after the angel.

The odd thing is that Percy St.-John came to Saint Ambrose on a windy November morning, much the same as I had. More or less left at the gate. After an odd commotion in the forecourt, the gate opened and there he stood — slender and carrying his pack, with ruddy cheeks and a full head of fair hair that seemed to stand up and then to go every which way at once. I could see he was feeling lost.

The thing people seem to notice about me is that I'm small for my age. The thing you notice about Percy is his eyes — large, dark eyes that can suddenly rake you with a piercing glance like you were something a dog had left at the doorstep.

Before Percy arrived, the most exciting events of my life happened when I was nine. It was then, you see, that I began to bump into things. I bumped into doors, walls, and furniture. But, when I bumped into old Brother Simon and caused him to drop a platter of the abbey's best stoneware, Father Abbot sent to Zurich for the famous oculist, Professor Dietrich. He examined me and some of the old monks and then fitted us with spectacles. At first, mine felt very thick and heavy on my nose, but I rejoiced that I no longer bumped into things and people.

2

I cannot remember much about my own history, but I remember the murder. The broken body of the little priest. And all the strange things that happened just before and after. But I'm getting ahead of myself. I guess I must begin at the beginning, where the nightmare that Percy and I lived together started.

You see, it all began that day, several months after Percy's arrival, as we scrubbed floors in the Scholarium. That's the monastery's great library. That was the day I began to see people who are not there. The day I began to hear the chorus of evil voices.

"Ouch! Each time I move, my knees feel like little pins are sticking them," said Percy, as he stopped scrubbing and glanced over at me. I could see the pain in his face. "Gabriel, we've washed most of the floor this afternoon. Time to unbend our legs. If we don't, we'll be walking like old Brother Paul the rest of our lives. Did you ever figure that Brother Paul probably got that way by scrubbing too many floors when he was young?"

Suddenly, he smiled. That deceptively angelic, gap-toothed grin that always signaled mischief. "No better way to stretch our legs than to climb the tower, eh?"

We dropped our brushes, sprang to our feet, and in the blink of an angel's eye we were scrambling up the long ladder toward the hatch that opens onto the roof of the abbey's great tower. One of our favorite places to go.

As soon as we stepped out, the wind caught our robes like sails, almost taking me off my feet. I closed my eyes and filled my lungs with air that smelled of the new life of early spring. In it was even the fragrance of flowers, though who knew from where.

Our abbey sits on a prominence, and, looking out from the north parapet, we could see clear across that broad valley in the high Alps watered by the River Aarn, all sparkling in the sunlight and washed in shades of blue and green. Across and beyond the valley there arise the ice-covered mountain peaks. Peering over the parapet we could see all the many buildings of the abbey itself — the church, Cloister*, the Dorter or dormitory, the Guest House beyond, and further still, we marveled at the most wondrous part of our abbey — the Tomb. The crypt of Saint Hilda of Braytherae, a twelfth-century Irish nun, lies within our monastery. This tomb is an object of pilgrimage by many who wish to obtain a cure by invoking the saint's name and begging God's mercy. The monastery is always host to numerous pilgrims, who sometimes stay with us for several weeks. Percy and I are assigned to care for their needs.

Holding out our arms to catch the wind, Percy and I glided to the south side of the parapet and gazed across the river to the village of Chaumont, nestled in the shadow of the abbey. In fact, the town and most of its surrounding farms and forests are the property of the abbey. Below us, wagons and people moved along the road that connects Zurich and western Switzerland with Austria to the east.

As a monk, I have never been permitted beyond the gate, and so I have often watched those people moving about and wondered about them — their lives, their homes, their shops, and businesses. I sometimes think that I find

Percy so interesting because he comes from the world beyond the gates. I remind myself too that the world beyond is filled with temptations to sin, and I fear that even to think about it may be sinful.

We glanced down upon the stone bridge that connects the monastery to the village across the river. To one side of that bridge stand the great iron gates of the abbey, proudly inscribed above with words of our patron saint, which are the motto of our community.

Veni redemptor Gentium

'O come Redeemer of the Earth'... what we monks look forward to with all our hearts. That gate stands guard over the great forecourt of the Church of St. Ambrose, where each Thursday the villagers hold their market.

As Percy gazed down, I found myself looking at him and wondering as I often did just why, or maybe how, he'd come to the monastery. He was about fifteen, I judged — close enough to my own age that Father Abbot had assigned me to be his mentor. I had not presumed to ask Percy about his past, though there was plenty of gossip about him among the brothers. The talk made him seem mysterious.

I am sure I had not heard all the rumors, but I knew the worst of it. Percy is a thief, the monks said. In fact, the brothers say that Percy, despite his age, is a famous thief and even, some said, an evil genius at stealing things — a sinful thing that will surely send him to everlasting hellfire if he does not repent.

Still, Percy seemed to me a good fellow. A little too lost in his own thoughts, most of the time and even given to brooding, but a good person nonetheless. I liked him and, in fact, I noticed that most of the monks did too, in spite of themselves. Since coming to the abbey he had been accepted as a lay-brother and had even impressed the older monks with his knowledge of Latin and Greek and his studies in the Scholarium. Oh yes, Percy St.-John was an odd fish alright. All this made me eager to know much more about him.

3

From the parapet, we surveyed the surrounding forest.

"Looks an evil place alright," said Percy, shaking his head.

"Oh yes," I agreed. "Dreadful. For hundreds of years, the folk hereabouts have feared the Forest of Ohme and have dreaded passing through it. Some say that just as God has claimed the prominence of the mountain for His holy monastery, Satan has claimed the lowly forest for his legion of demons."

Percy cocked his head and eyed me sympathetically, the way he often does. I continued, "Just last month, I heard Brother Felix say that a farmer... poor fellow... who dared to follow a straying cow into the forest found the unfortunate beast, its carcass being fed upon by winged demons, who fluttered away at his approach, cursing him and God. Imagine that, Percy. They were cursing God."

"Gabriel, if you'll pardon me for saying so, that's a lot of monk piffle. You've got to get a grip, m'lad, or you'll be a raving lunatic in only a few years. Living in this place as long as you have can do strange things to a young mind."

I ignored Percy's sinful attitude, as I often do, and instead continued to gaze out at the mountains. When I turned again to Percy, he was standing rigid, his eyes closed and his arms at his sides.

At first, I thought he was shamming. Making more fun of my beliefs. He was fond of doing such things. "Percy! Stop shamming," I demanded. Nothing.

I don't know why but just then I turned to look behind me, and there stood an old man — dressed in a rough wool tunic, with a rope cinch and a rough-made wooden cross on a leather string about his neck. His long white hair and beard radiated out from his scowling face. His fierce eyes seemed to be on fire. His arms were outstretched. At me!

My blood ran cold and the look of him so frightened me that I fell to my knees. Just then the old man rose up above the roof by a meter or more and hovered in the air before me. Maybe it's God the Father, I thought. The old man looked like I often imagined God must look.

I closed my eyes, hoping he would disappear and prove I was having a dream. No good. When I opened my eyes, he was still there, his fiery eyes still fixed on me and looking even angrier.

Now standing, I too began to rise off the roof. The frightful old man kept his gaze riveted on me, as I began to hover, first above the tower roof and then slowly out beyond the parapet, high above the forecourt. I knew that somehow it was the force of the old man's gaze that had lifted me off the roof. I wanted to close my eyes, but couldn't. For some reason, I was compelled to experience the full fright of drifting high above the pavement below, knowing that I would surely fall to my death.

Then there came from deep within the old man a low, guttural voice, which said only one word: "*Cavefacio!*" A word I did not understand.

Once this was said, the old man seemed to lose energy. He closed his eyes. Then repeated, only now in a lower, less angry voice, "*Cavefacio.*"

The old man's loss of energy allowed me to close my eyes and when I reopened them, I found myself kneeling on the roof, still terrified.

I turned to look at Percy, to see if he'd witnessed the same thing — heard the strange word — but he remained rigid, his eyes closed.

When I turned once more the old man was gone.

"Why are you kneeling, Gabriel?" I heard Percy ask. I swung around with a start and came to my feet.

"Percy! Did you see him? Hear him?"

"See who?"

"The old man with the white beard."

"You saw an old man? Where?" he asked, looking over the parapet.

"Yes," I said, insisting. "Here. On the tower. An angry old man who hovered.... Looked like God the Father."

Percy's face suddenly filled with disbelief. "Gabriel, you've been having one of those monkish visions that people who live in places like this often have. It's a trick your mind plays on you. Happens all the time in monasteries, eh?"

All that gave me to know that Percy was not going to believe me. So I decided merely to ask him something I did not understand.

"Percy, what does *Cavefacio* mean? I know it's Latin, but I am a simple speaker and it's not a word I know."

Percy raised his chin and looked at me differently, somehow. Strangely. As if I'd said something I was not supposed to know.

"It's an odd and very ancient way of saying *Caveo* — Beware," he explained.

"Oh."

Percy continued to eye me strangely, in a sidelong way. Meanwhile, there was something very calming in Percy's explanation, and I was no longer frightened. It troubled me that I did not understand why I should see something that Percy did not see. Why I should be warned to 'Beware,' when others were not. What, I wondered, was happening to me? I decided to say no more and tell no one of the strange man, lest everyone should think I was going mad.

Chapter Two

Wherein Percy is Accused

1

Just then the great bell began to ring, almost shaking us off our feet. Percy glanced at me wide-eyed. "Vespers (4.30 p.m.), and we'll be late again for sure!" he shouted, covering his ears with his hands.

I couldn't hear him above the noise of the bell, but there was no need to tell me what to do. We dashed for the hatch and slid down the ladder at a speed only a little short of a free fall. I went first and I remembered thinking that if I stopped Percy would surely crash into me and knock me loose.

Once at the foot of the tower, we scurried across the church and into the chapel, where the monks had gathered ahead of us. Once again Percy and I brought up the rear, under the disapproving eyes of the older monks. We sat without looking up.

There was already a special excitement in the air. It was the Day of Ashes* and the entire monastery was entering into the joy of anticipating the day of Our Lord's Resurrection. Father Abbot arrived a little late — more's the relief to Percy and me — and as he took his seat, Prior Oswald entered, looking around, his eyes wide, and it seemed to me, distressed.

The Prior is a tall, bulky man with a long nose, small mouth, and large ears. He has a way of towering over others and looking down his nose in the most unpleasant way. I hesitate to say it, but it has always seemed to me that

Prior Oswald is excessively proud of his place as second only to Father Abbot in the leadership of our community, and he makes no secret that he hopes God will place the Abbot's cross upon him someday.

Oswald rushed to Abbot Bartholomew's side and began to whisper excitedly in his ear. Father's Abbot's face grew white, and his eyes bulged.

Father Abbot's expression grew more pained the longer Prior Oswald whispered. When the Prior had finished Father Abbot motioned him to take his place, and from that time on we chanted* our prayers. When we'd finished and prepared to return to our work, Abbot Bartholomew stood. "Brothers," he said, grim-faced, "a terrible thing has happened. One of the books of our Scholarium is missing. Sadly, the missing book is the rarest and most treasured of our collection, because we know it once belonged to our dear Saint Hilda."

The brothers gasped and fell to puzzled murmuring, but none spoke. The Abbot, his face long, pale, and grim, said no more but dismissed us to our duties with a wave of his hand.

2

Later, after supper, Prior Oswald came to the table where Percy sat, and I heard him say, in a stern voice — Prior Oswald's voice always reminds me of curdled milk — "The Abbot wishes to see you, Brother Percy." It's an odd thing to be summoned by the Abbot at that time of day, and because of all the commotion earlier, I was sure all the brothers wondered, as I did, whatever was afoot.

Percy told me later that he had to get up his courage as he approached the Abbot's study — a small, bare room adjacent to a bedchamber. He knocked gently at the door and heard from inside the stern command, "Come in."

"You wished to see me, Father Abbot?" Percy asked, his eyes darting from corner to corner of the room.

Abbot Bartholomew — a tall, slender man, with a long, angular face and a bald dome of a head — stood as Percy entered, his hands tucked in the sleeves of his black robe. His small mouth puckered, and his cold blue eyes seemed to pin Percy's feet to the floor.

"Please sit," he said, frowning and motioning with a sweep of his hand to a chair near the crackling hearth. When Percy had taken the chair, the Abbot continued to stand. "I have summoned you, Brother Percy, because of the missing book."

"Yes, Father Abbot?" Percy asked.

"Prior Oswald tells me you've often used the Scholarium and have customarily studied in the same room where the book was kept."

"I have often used the Scholarium, Father Abbot. I read both Greek and Latin, you see, and I've been making some notes on — "

"Yes, yes — well... that's all well and good," the Abbot cut him short. "But it's the missing book that concerns me just now."

"Yes, sir?" Percy blinked and swallowed, not liking the way the conversation was going.

"Oswald testifies that you were the last person to leave the Scholarium last evening, just before Compline (6 p.m.). He had some work to do elsewhere, so he asked you to lock up and to return the key to him as we gathered to pray."

"Yes, that is so," said Percy.

"I will be plainspoken with you, Percy St.-John," said the Abbot, now frowning and his voice cold. "Given what I know of your past and the troubles you've caused before coming here, I must suspect that you are the thief. I give you fair warning. You'll not be able to take the book you've stolen from the monastery, so you best return it to me now. I'll make no further fuss about the matter, though I will, of course, inform your French employers and tell them you are to be expelled from the abbey."

"But Father Abbot," Percy protested, rising from his chair, "I have not taken the book! I'm innocent! I don't even know what book is missing!"

"Come, come, boy. You needn't play the innocent with me. It must be you who took our book, and I tell you now I mean to have it from you," he said, stiffening his neck and crossing his arms, as his eyes narrowed.

There was a long silence. Percy's mouth suddenly ran dry with fear.

"Very well, Brother Percy," the Abbot continued. "I'll not confine you just now, because we have yet to make a thorough search of your things. The book could not have been taken from the monastery, because no one has come or gone since it went missing. We will find it where you've hidden it — you may be sure of that — so at least we will have the book and the proof of your guilt. Now go. Continue your duties, but be warned," he said, his eyes cold. "I know what you've done."

Percy stood and left the Abbot's study, without another word in his own defense. He could see Father Abbot had already declared him guilty and would listen to none of his claims otherwise. "Convicted without a trial," Percy told me later, "and nothing I could do about it."

In the narrow passage just outside, Percy found Prior Oswald, looking down his nose with a scowling face. Brother Oswald never smiles and always speaks of discipline and penance. He is also one of those who speak often of God's wrath.

"Return that book, Brother Percy," he said menacingly. "Repent your sin," he added and continued to glare, as Percy made his way down the passage. From Prior Oswald's attitude, Percy knew that few would believe him and he could only escape the accusation by finding and returning the book himself. At least, that's what he had decided by the time he descended the night stairs and once again drew a deep breath in the crisp air of the Cloister.

While Percy was with the Abbot, I found myself thinking how frightening it had been to see Percy in a trance and then the old man who looked like an angry God. Now, I dared not tell anyone what I'd seen on the tower, lest they should declare Percy possessed by Satan. I also still feared they might think me insane. As I walked along the dark passage to my cell in the Dorter, with those thoughts dancing in my head, I heard a low growl — like the snarl of a wolf.

I stopped to look behind me, and it was then I heard it for the first time — the faint sound of a chorus*, chanting an evil-sounding hymn. It grew louder and louder as I hurried to my cell, but when I threw myself on my cot and covered my head with my pillow, it stopped.

3

The horror of his meeting with Father Abbot and then Prior Oswald left Percy feeling as if he'd just escaped from a monster. The words "Return that book!" echoed in his mind all night and even as he came into the Refectory the next morning for breakfast. His face looked to me even more dismal, and I saw too that the other monks were casting secret glances at him, just as they had done earlier, at Lauds (5:00-6:00 a.m.). The thick fog of suspicion had fallen over Brother Percy, and there was no defending against it. Prior Oswald had spread the news of Percy's "crime" among the brothers. I could not remember such whispering and disturbance in the abbey — not since three years earlier when old Brother Valerian, the gatekeeper, had confronted a snarling demon, roaming about the forecourt in the small hours of a December morning. At the time, I had doubted Brother Valerian's story, but now I was not so sure.

When Percy took his place at a table, none of the other monks took a seat beside him, or even near his place. I decided to show my disdain for their behaviour. I moved immediately to sit directly across from Brother Percy. I smiled at him too, so everyone could see.

When the Abbot and Prior had arrived and were seated, the brothers who serve meals came with our bowls and cups, and the brother charged with reading the Scripture at that meal commenced his reading. There is no talking permitted at mealtime, except by the reader, and so afterward I followed Percy to the nearby Locutory, where speaking is permitted at some times of the day.

"Brother Percy, the monks are saying the Abbot summoned you because you surely took the missing book. When I passed your cell earlier Prior Oswald and Brother Jean-Baptiste were in there — searching it," I whispered.

"Yes, I figured everyone would know by now. Well, I have nothing to do with the missing book. No one has even bothered to tell me what book I am supposed to have stolen. What is this book, exactly? I've never heard of it."

"That's because you were not permitted to know of it. Only those who have been a monk for ten years are permitted to know of it, and only the most senior monks are permitted to see it."

"What is it? What's it called?"

"It has no name that I ever knew, and so the monks call it merely the *Cronica mysteria*."

"*The Chronicle of Secrets*? What's it about?"

"I don't know. Never seen it myself... at least not that I know. I might have dusted it when I've cleaned the Scholarium. Oh no... maybe I wasn't permitted even to tell you the name of the thing."

"Listen, Gabriel," said Percy, taking my forearm. "You seem to want to help me, and I'm dashed grateful for that, but if you wish to help, you mustn't hold back. I can't get myself out of this mess if I don't know everything about the crime I'm accused of committing. I must find that book... to clear my good name."

"But you don't have a good name, Percy. In fact, your name is — "

"Yes, well, putting all that aside, I've got to have that book to stay out of prison."

When Percy said the word prison, a look came in his eyes that I'd not seen before. Percy was frightened.

"Yes, I guess you're right there. And I do wish to help because I do not believe you are guilty, Brother Percy. Even though you are a troubled soul because of your past thievery. Still...."

"Let's have it, Gabriel. No holding back," he insisted, frowning. "What do the monks say about that book?"

"The book is a manuscript of the twelfth century, in the time of our beloved Saint Hilda, as Father Abbot said. It's said to have been brought here, from Ireland, by Saint Hilda herself. That's why it's so revered. It was the property of our saint." I crossed myself.

"I see. What's this book, precisely then? What does it say?"

"I have no idea. No one has ever told me."

"But, what do the brother monks say it's about?"

"It's in the title. It is said to convey secret knowledge. Frightening secrets, Percy. Only one as saintly as our dear Hilda would dare to read it, they say."

"What frightful secrets?"

"I don't know. Just secrets, I guess. Frightful secrets, they say, and that's enough to keep me away from the thing. If I ever come face-to-face with it, I will surely close my eyes and pray." I crossed myself again.

Percy frowned and shot me a disappointed glance. He fell silent, too. It was a thick kind of silence, like the gruel that's served in our Refectory. Then he said, "Very well... but one thing is clear now."

"What?" I asked, thinking that almost nothing was clear to me.

"If I don't find that book, I'm in serious trouble. Big trouble. A peaceful year in this abbey was my last chance. If I don't clear myself, the people who sent me here — the French mainly — will lock me away somewhere and forget about me." Then he repeated, mainly to himself — "and forget about me."

That left me to wonder why exactly Percy had been sent to our monastery, and who were those French people he was talking about?

Chapter Three
Wherein Mr. Tandy Dreams

New York City. Four Months Earlier
Christmas Eve, 1910

1

Does it matter... what I have to do to get it? No, 'course not. I'll kill and worse, right enough. Getting it's everything to me... everything... the end of my dreams. The making of m'fortune.

How much'll that be, in the end, eh? Riches beyond m'wildest dreams, I'll wager. Him that wants it'll pay a king's ransom to get it, they say. Aye, a king's ransom.

2

And so Mr. Tandy dreamed of riches, as the wheels of his hansom cab clattered over wet cobbles, rolling through foggy, dimly-lit backstreets, past warehouses, and shabby shops, near the old Brooklyn Docks. Mr. Tandy — a short, chubby man, with a large, crumpled nose and pink face — smiled. After a life of danger, cheating, and murder, his heart soared on one thought. He was on his way to meet the man who would make him rich — very rich.

The cab drew up at a corner where a gaslight bathed its surroundings for only a few yards, and beyond, there was only the misty darkness.

"Wait for me. I'll only be a bit," said Tandy, as he stepped to the curb and tossed a coin to the cabby. The driver nodded, his eyes darting nervously from side to side, afraid to wait alone in such a place. Tandy turned and disappeared into the darkness of a narrow alley, past dustbins and scattered trash, moving toward a dim light at the distant end. A sudden wind whipped through the alley, stirring a flutter of old newspapers and debris. Deeper into the alley, the stink of garbage, decaying rodents, and cat urine filled Tandy's nostrils. He retched, then put his scarf to his nose as he knocked twice on the filthy door beneath the light. The door cracked an inch. An angry, gravelly voice demanded, "What?"

"I'm here to see him. I was told he's expecting me," said Tandy, forcing a smile.

A pair of small, birdlike eyes peered through a slightly larger crack. The door creaked open, into a long, dim passageway, with peeling yellow paint on the walls.

"That way," said a short, fat man with bushy eyebrows, nodding down the passage. "Down there to the door at the end. Knock once. Just once, mind ye. He don't like no more."

Tandy smiled nervously and did as he was told. At the door, his knock brought a clear, commanding reply. "Enter!"

3

The door opened into a large, ornate room — a study or library of sorts, richly decorated with polished woodwork, fine drapery of red damask brocade, and mahogany furnishings. Bookshelves, filled with volumes bound in fine leather, lined two walls, while on a table in the middle of the room there lay several large books that were clearly very old. The room was lit by a single lamp resting on a large desk. And behind the desk, his face hidden in shadows, sat the man himself, his long, pale, skeletal hands folded comfortably across his stomach.

"Ah, Mr. Tandy. How very nice you've come."

Tandy extended a hand, but the man in the shadows ignored it. Mr. Tandy drew it back, a little embarrassed.

"You needn't come farther into the room," said the man, his voice weak. "I can see you well enough where you are."

"As you say, sir," said Tandy, standing to attention. There followed a long, unnatural silence. In that silence, Tandy could hear only the labored breathing of the man in the shadows, and somehow, the gurgling unnerved him.

"I was instructed to come," Tandy finally decided to say. "But I do not know your proper name, sir."

The man gave a faint laugh. "Bloodworth, Mr. Tandy. Cidolfus Bloodworth, and so pleased to finally meet you." There was a sweetness in the voice that somehow disturbed Mr. Tandy. Disturbed and frightened him.

Just then, the man in the chair erupted in coughing — the deep, rasping, guttural hacking of failing lungs. The fit lasted a minute or more. When it subsided, Mr. Bloodworth leaned back, resting his head on the back of his chair, as if exhausted. Tandy waited awkwardly for him to continue.

As Mr. Bloodworth started to speak again there came from an adjacent room a loud scream, then shouting, followed by anguished pleading. A man, begging for his life.

Bloodworth gave a quick, sidelong glance at a door to his right, then turned to Tandy, a wolfish smile on his thin lips.

"A bit of business we are... er... we are finalizing tonight. Another matter entirely, you see."

Tandy swallowed hard and nodded his understanding, then waited for Bloodworth to continue.

"Then you are ready to undertake this task I have for you, eh? You're prepared to travel, and you know precisely what you are to do?" he asked, his voice even weaker.

"Yes, sir. Your man instructed me. He told me you'd give the final nod and instructions this evening, and then I'd be off."

"Yes, well... you come highly recommended, Mr. Tandy. You should do nicely for what I have in mind, though it's a mission of a special... dare I say, a unique kind." He coughed a little, then spit into his handkerchief.

"Yes, I could tell that from my briefing, sir, but there remains the matter of — "

"Ah, yes — you wish to know about your pay, eh? Oh yes, you must be rewarded for success, if you get it for me. Oh yes." Mr. Bloodworth chuckled.

"And that is — ?" Tandy pressed.

Taking a thick envelope from the desk drawer, Bloodworth tossed it on the desk, in arm's reach of Tandy.

"Take it and count it if you wish. It's a third of what's coming."

Tandy did as he was told, thumbing through the banknotes. Then he smiled.

"Notice your tickets are in there as well. You'll get the rest...."

Bloodworth paused to cough, though not as violently as before, and then continued. "...You'll get the rest when you deliver the goods. A word of caution, however."

"Sir?"

"You must get it! You must!" he repeated, slamming the fist that held the handkerchief on the desk. Then, he fell into another fit of coughing and wheezing. Tandy stood by calmly until Mr. Bloodworth had regained his composure. "Don't fail me, I beg you. It's as much as your life if you fail me, Mr. Tandy. I am not a man to accept failure, you see."

Tandy swallowed hard yet again but then smiled. "No fear, sir. I'll not fail you... or m'self," he said, sliding the envelope into his coat's inside pocket.

"Good. Very good. Now go, and see you get it."

Tandy turned and departed. As he closed the door and walked up the dingy passage toward the fat man, violent coughing erupted from behind him.

Chapter Four
Wherein We Meet the Angry Girl

Monastery of St. Ambrose, 3 April 1911

1

The day after he was accused, Percy and I took up one of our usual duties, mopping and cleaning in the Guest House, where the abbey's pilgrims reside. As usual, the Guest House was full, mainly of those seeking a cure. St. Hilda was herself lame and was said to have a special love and pity for those like her, who suffer from deformities. She had worked miracles for many who'd come as pilgrims, they said, even for those with illnesses thought to be incurable. The Easter season always seemed to bring even more pilgrims, who filled our Guest House as well as the hostels and inns in the village of Chaumont.

The weeks after the Day of Ashes were always especially solemn in our abbey, as the brothers offered extra prayers for the pilgrims. The atmosphere of the place seemed to grow somber and even grim, as we awaited the day of the dreadful Crucifixion.

Percy and I stayed busy most days, caring for the needs of the many guests. Those pilgrims, like all strangers, interested me. I found myself wondering often about their lives and where they'd come from. Some came as families, with a sick person in search of a cure. Others were what we called faith pilgrims — those making a gesture of faith, but not seeking a cure. Some were on a long journey between holy places, stopping to pay homage to St. Hilda on their way. How wonderful, I dreamed, it must be to make a pilgrimage.

The family of Monsieur François Dugard — the well-known Paris anti-quarian — were our most distinguished pilgrims. Madame Marie-Claire Dugard and her husband had come seeking a cure for their daughter, Elizabeth — a lame girl who walked with a crutch. Percy and I agreed that Mademoiselle Elizabeth was very pretty, what with her long blonde hair, large eyes, and rosy cheeks. I was more concerned than Percy that noticing such things might be sinful.

The other cure seekers were English. Lady Dorothy Everson appeared to be about twenty-five years and pale. Her nurse, Mrs. Martha Downey and her aunt, Lady Jane Marbury, accompanied her everywhere, most often pushing her in a Bathchair. Lady Jane, a stout and frowning woman, demanded a great deal of service and complained often. It was whispered that the young woman was suffering a consumptive disease that would surely take her life.

Among the faith pilgrims, there were all kinds. Mr. Hugo Westerman was said to be a very rich English man of business, and he seemed so. He spoke often with Mr. Lucas Covington, an American who Prior Oswald referred to as 'the millionaire.' He too seemed to have no malady.

An old German professor, Herr Doktor Helmut Eidenbuch and his two students, Herr Schmitt and Herr Becker, had traveled from Dresden. They puz-zled us, because they did not seem to be devout Catholics, nor did they seem to be seeking a cure.

Father Enrico Solari, who had come from Turin, seemed an odd person. Young, shabbily dressed, and sullen, no one knew if he was seeking a cure or not, but Percy and I agreed we did not much like him. He walked with a limp and a cane, so we assumed he wished to be cured, but strangely, he seldom attended the special prayers of those who did.

2

"Boy, come here," commanded an angry voice from behind me. Percy and I looked at each other and then turned together to see that it was the French girl, Elizabeth, wearing a scowl on her face. This was the first time she'd said anything to either of us. Percy had said that she was 'snooty' — an English word meaning arrogant, he explained.

"Oui," said Percy, as the girl approached. Because we worked at the Guest House, Brother Percy and I had permission to speak to the pilgrims, if they spoke to us first.

"This blanket you've given me is filthy," she protested, glaring at Percy with a forceful eye. "Look here, at the cat hair on it. Do you use it for your cats and then share it with me?" she scolded.

Percy looked closely at the blanket. "But, where are the hairs, Mademoiselle?" he asked, looking up. "I cannot see even one."

"There!" she pointed. "A half-blind imbecile could see it!"

Percy looked up. "Yes... I see it now. But, it's... it's only one hair. Only one."

"What of it? It's filthy. Take it back and bring me another," she huffed. "And this time, try to find one that's clean. You do know the meaning of clean, don't you?" She stiffened her neck.

Percy and I exchanged glances, and I knew I was about to witness one of Brother Percy's painful efforts to retain his monastic humility. I shuddered a little to remember that Percy sometimes failed those tests, and so I closed my eyes and braced for the explosion.

After a moment of silence, my mouth fell open just a little, when I heard Percy say, "Of course, Mademoiselle. I will return with another, clean blanket, in a moment."

"Good," she said, with a smirk. "See that you return quickly." She walked away, leaning on her crutch and dragging her foot a little as she walked. When she'd moved out of earshot, I said quietly, "Percy, I am staggered with admiration at your Christian forbearance. Even Timothy is praising you."

Then, looking after her, he said more to himself than to me, "That arrogant witch deserves a good spank — ." Not finishing, he turned quickly to me, a question on his face. "Timothy? Who's Timothy?"

I gasped to realize that, in my dumbfounded admiration for Percy, I'd let slip my deepest secret — something I'd not told anyone, and especially now a well-known sinner and former scoundrel such as Percy.

"Oh, it's n-n-no one," I lied, "and you are right about her. Her parents have f-f-failed t-t-to encourage a proper Catholic spirit in her. She has a terrible disposition, that girl does."

"Who is Timothy?" Percy persisted. "You're stuttering, Gabriel. You always do that when you're nervous — and when you're lying."

I knew he would wheedle it out of me, so I decided to trust him. After all, Percy had become my closest friend.

"Percy, you must promise to keep what I tell you in the strictest confidence between us. Promise?"

He gave me an impatient toss of his eyes upward. "Yes, of course. I promise. Who is Timothy? There's no Brother Timothy here. Someone from the village? And don't lie. I'll know if you lie. You're among the poorest liars I've ever met, and I have dealt with some champion liars in my time. In fact, it's part of my business to associate with such people."

He was right. "Very well, I'll trust you with this most sacred information."

Percy stiffened and raised his chin, then looked down his nose. "Sacred information?"

"Timothy is my... he is... I mean to say, Timothy is my guardian angel."

Percy's mouth dropped open, and then he let out a laugh so loud it caused some of the pilgrims in the courtyard to look our way. I was offended, and he could see it.

"Sorry, Brother Gabriel, but you shocked me. You promised not to lie, and then you just stepped back and let go a big one. That lie was so big, I could see it leave your body and float off toward the mountains, like a dark cloud. Look! There it goes!" He pointed, still laughing.

"You are mistaken, Percy. It was not a lie, and I don't care if you believe me or not. I told you, and there it is."

"Good Lord," he said, now looking in my eyes strangely. "You are telling the truth. You must tell me more about this imaginary friend of yours," he invited, lowering his voice to a confidential murmur.

"He is not imaginary. He's real. As real as you or me. I see him. I hear him. And, I know who he is."

"You see him? Do you see him right now?" Percy asked, in a doubtful tone.

"Yes."

"Where?"

"What?"

"I mean, where is he right now?"

I glanced up and over Percy's shoulder. "He's standing just behind you. And I can tell by his face, he's none too happy with me for telling you about him. I expect he'll give me some spiritual advice later."

Percy turned around quickly as if to catch sight of Timothy. While he did so, he asked, "What does this guardian angel of yours look like? Long white robe, golden sash, wings, eh?

"No. Not at all," I said, frowning.

When he turned back to me his eyes narrowed and his lips pursed.

"What then?"

"He wears a proper dark suit, like the rich American, and a bowler hat. Carries a very nice cane too, and always wears spats."

Percy let out another laugh.

"A natty chap. I'll give him credit for that."

Then, looking earnestly at me, he continued: "Gabriel, you must get a grip on yourself, my lad. Sometimes your monkishness is just a little frightening. This place can do strange things to a fellow's mind, you know."

I did not reply, because I could see that Timothy was motioning me to let it drop.

"Well, I must go fetch another blanket," he finally said.

In the meantime, I continued our cleaning. Percy soon returned with the new blanket, but instead of leaving it for the girl at the Guest House, he found Elizabeth waiting on the steps, frowning and with her arms crossed.

"Took you long enough," she rebuked, as he handed her the new blanket.

At first taken aback by the girl's surly attitude, but sympathetic with her situation, Percy did not reply in kind. Instead, he merely said, "Oui, Mademoiselle," and turned to leave.

Apparently still angry, she continued, "You're the English brother... the one they say took the book." He turned, surprised that even the pilgrims were gossiping about the missing book and the Abbot's suspicions. His eyes flashed.

"How'd you know that?" he asked.

"Papa learned it from Sister Rose, the Irish nun who just arrived, and she had it from one of the monks she talks to."

Percy decided not to satisfy the girl's appetite for gossip, said nothing, and turned again to leave.

"Well, did you take it?" she asked after him.

By now Percy's temper was rising. He turned, frowning.

"Mademoiselle would be well-advised to look to her cure and leave the gossip about me well enough alone."

"You're a strange sort of monk," she said, looking at him with a questioning eye.

"I'm not a monk. I'm a lay-brother, and even that's none of my doing."

"What? You mean you are being held here by force?"

"Yes. In a way."

"Well then, whose doing was that? That you are here against your will?" she asked, doubtfully.

"Long story, but the short answer is the Deuxième Bureau* put me here, for a year, as a reform program, you might say."

This was the first time I'd heard of this Deuxième whatever, and I didn't know what to make of it. The girl did, however, because her mouth dropped open at least an inch.

"You mean to say the French Intelligence Service put you here?" she said as if disbelieving.

"But why the Deuxième Bureau? You're English."

"You might say I am a ward of the DB," Percy explained. "I work for them on special projects, and they take care of me. At least, that's the way it's supposed to work. Trouble is, I ventured off on my own to do a bit of freelancing — that involved stealing one of Leonardo's better paintings — and I got caught. Then I ended up in here."

"And just what is it you do for the Deuxième Bureau?" she asked, with a doubting look and one hand on her hip.

Percy hesitated. "What d'ye think? I steal things."

"What!"

"Listen, Mademoiselle," Percy said, impatiently. "I keep saying things very clearly and you keep saying 'What!'– as if you didn't hear me. Is something wrong with your hearing... or with my French?"

"No. Your French is excellent, and I hear perfectly well, merci, but...."

"Yes, I steal things! I'm good at it too," he insisted. "It's what I do. It's my trade, you might say, and I enjoy it like nothing else. When you are like me, you can practice your trade in one of two ways. You can be a lone thief, do a bit of good business, but ultimately end up in a place like this, or worse. Or, you can work for some government or other and maybe stay out of prison. In my case, I work for the French, but I sometimes hire out to the Special Branch* too, because the English are now working closely with the French, thanks to the alliance. You know, the Triple Entente*?"

Her eyes bulged. "Mère de Dieu! You're a spy!"

"No. I told you. I'm a thief. I just work for spies. One in particular, in fact."

"Who is he?"

"Can't tell you, but I wish he was here now. He'd know how to get me out of this pickle. It's going to take me a while to figure it out on my own."

As Percy turned once again to leave, she said, "You haven't asked me about my foot. Aren't you curious?"

"No. It's clear you're lame, and I tend to mind my own business. Besides, at the moment I have my own problems. Au revoir, Mademoiselle."

"No, wait!" she demanded. Percy turned back as if to see what troubled her now.

I was almost shocked, then, to hear her ask something I'd always wondered about Percy but had hesitated to ask him. I didn't want to snoop, you see.

"How came you to be out on your own, making your way as a thief? And so young too," she asked, as if she were ten years older than us.

"Orphaned," he said tersely.

"Oh?" She encouraged him to explain. He looked at her, his eyes as sad as I had ever seen them. The girl sat down on a nearby bench, as though prepared to hear a long story. Percy hesitated, but then we took a seat facing her.

"My mother died when I was a baby. Never knew her. Reared by my father, who was a vicar — an Anglican pastor — in a small village in Surrey. Not much pay. We were always struggling. We had only each other in all the world, and we were the best of friends. I loved him like no one else, and he loved me too," he said in an insisting way.

"Oh," she said, sympathetically. "But, what happened? Why are you not still there?"

Percy looked at her a long moment, and in a strange way. I expected he'd tell her to mind her own business.

"When I was nine years old... one night... as he returned home from visiting a sick parishioner, he was set upon by thieves. Imagine, a man who was always the poorest of the poor was attacked by thieves... thieves... they... they beat him. Killed him. Right there, on the road," Percy said, lowering his voice to a near-whisper.

The French girl and I were both struck silent. He continued.

"No family... least, none that wanted me... so, I was sent to an orphanage, near London. I lived there a year. A horrible place, where I was always cold or steaming and where the food often had maggots in it. One of the lads there taught me to pick locks, and that was the making of me, you might say. I learned that I had a gift for opening things. Not a lock in the orphanage I couldn't open." He smiled.

"You ran away?"

"As soon as I could, and got m'self a job as a shop boy for a locksmith. It was there I finished my education. Soon, I was ready to go out on my own, and I've made my way ever since. The orphanage taught me what it is to be locked up, and I never want that again." Percy's face looked very sad.

We sat in silence for a long while, until Elizabeth rose, now prepared to go to the Guest House. As she took up her crutch, she seemed to have a second thought, turned and looked at Percy in the oddest way. She started to say something but decided against it, and then she left.

3

Percy and I returned to sweeping the Guest House stairs. He seemed troubled. I thought maybe it was the angry girl and all the questions she'd asked, but it wasn't.

"Gabriel, I'm sure the Abbot and Oswald will soon summon the canton police, and they'll likely drag me off to the nearest jail. If I'm locked away I'll never clear myself, and likely as not the jolly old Deuxième Bureau will get fed up and leave me in jail to rot." Percy's face grew very worried. "I could never stand to be locked up again. I think I would die in prison."

"And whoever took the book will get away," I added, changing the subject from prison. "But who took it? Where shall we start?"

"I've been considering that too, and I'm thinking it was Dugard."

"That girl's papa? The famous auctioneer?"

"Of course. He's a natural suspect. Consider. He is probably Europe's biggest and richest antiquities dealer, and do you know what his specialty is?"

"No."

"Rare books! That's what."

"Good Heavens! I see what you mean."

"Good. And while you're catching on, just look at that daughter of his. Now there's a girl who'd — "

Before Percy could finish his thought, an icy voice came from behind us. I guess it's just me, but people always seem to sneak up on me.

"How dare you!" The voice was familiar, but now even icier. We turned to see Mademoiselle Elizabeth on the stairs. She'd returned for some reason, and her eyes were flashing anger at Percy. She was holding her crutch in such a way, I thought she'd take a swing at him.

"How dare you accuse my papa of your crime, you scoundrel!" she said, even colder. "He's the most honest man in Paris — in France, even — damn you! You have no cause to say what you say. You keep your evil little mind away from my papa!"

The girl's eyes raged at Percy, but he was having none of it.

"That may be so, Mademoiselle, but I don't know your father. I only know that I'm being hounded for a theft I didn't do, and he's at least one of the people who might well have done it."

Rather than be a witness to more of the girl's anger, I moved off to continue my work and left Percy behind to calm her as best he could. I figured she might pick up a rock or stick and go after someone, and I was eager to be out of danger. I am not a coward, but it has always seemed that a proper attitude recommends prudence in all things.

The girl's face relaxed a bit, and the red rage in her eyes gave way to a frigid glare. "Very well, you'll see for yourself that François Dugard is an honest man. Do not spend your valuable time chasing after him, while the real thief escapes with the book. All the monks are saying you took it because you are a well-known thief. You see, they are suspicious of you, just like you are suspicious of Papa."

"Very well," said Percy. "Let's agree that I'll not pursue your papa, for the moment, and you'll tell me all you hear about the theft. Agreed?"

"Oui, d'accord," she said. "Bon. My parents are enough distressed already, without your vile accusations."

"Distressed? Why?"

She looked down. "They're both anxious for me to... well, they both believe I will have a cure. That's why they're here, you see. Especially Mama — she's very spiritual in that way. Mumbles prayers over me constantly. She's distressed just now because we pilgrims are kept at such a distance from the Saint. Not allowed beyond the iron fence and gate to touch the Saint's crypt, you see. Mama says it would be so much better if I could touch the Saint's tomb."

"The monks say the fence is to protect the pilgrims. Haven't you heard about the force?" Percy asked.

She looked puzzled. "No. The force?"

"Yes. Saint Hilda is protected by a mysterious force. The monks fear even to touch the crypt themselves because they believe the force will strike them dead, especially if they are sinful. That's why the tall fence is there."

She turned to me, nearby. "Brother Gabriel. You mean no one may touch the crypt? No one may go in it?"

"Well, I guess Father Abbot could, but he doesn't. No one does. There's no need, and then... well, there's the force to be feared," I explained. "I guess even Father Abbot fears it."

Percy nodded. "So you can assure your dear mama that the fence and gate are for her own good. Yours too." The girl did not reply, but limped away toward the Refectory on her crutch, as we looked on after her.

"She's one to avoid," I reflected, knowing that some pilgrims were difficult to please and were best left to themselves.

"Yes, I suppose so," Percy said, as he continued to look on after her. "Perhaps."

Chapter Five
Wherein the German Student Vanishes

1

By next morning, I was sure most of the brothers and pilgrims believed Percy had stolen the book. Worse, I assumed Father Abbot would summon the police to take him away. It was just then, however, that something happened, which shook everyone's confidence in their belief about Percy and caused yet another disturbance in our abbey.

Just after Lauds, as Percy and I joined the brothers for breakfast and waited silently for the Scripture reading, Brother Jean-Baptiste scurried into the Refectory and whispered in Father Abbot's ear. The Abbot's face turned white, his eyes bulged. Prior Oswald leaned-in to hear what was said. He frowned, then his mouth fell open. Father Abbot rose and hurriedly followed Brother Jean-Baptiste from the room.

Whispers went round the room — up one table and down the next — in a whirlwind of gossip, never mind that we were bound to silence at meals. "The German student is missing," Brother Felix whispered to me, loud enough for Percy to hear. "Vanished. In the night." Oh my! I thought. I turned to Percy. "Yes, vanished," Felix repeated, "like smoke in the wind."

"Maybe it was one of the German students who took the book? And now, he's run away!" I exclaimed in a low voice.

Percy said nothing. Instead, he looked blankly in the middle-distance, as a torrent of whispers swirled around the dining tables.

"Now, everyone will suspect the student, for sure," I said, more to myself than to Percy.

Prior Oswald glared and banged a heavy fist on his table to quiet the whispering and mumbling. No more was said, but I noticed many of the brothers looked occasionally at Percy.

All that morning, as Percy and I cleaned the Guest House, I thought alternately about the book and the missing student. We heard from Brother Pierre that the Abbot had questioned Herr Becker about his missing friend and Becker said Herr Schmitt had been distressed for some time. I watched Percy every chance I got, to see if he had thought of something, but I could see nothing in his face to tell me he had. Just as we finished, the French girl appeared, as if from nowhere, and tapped Percy on the shoulder. For a lame girl with a crutch, she was certainly good at sneaking up on us. Percy turned with a gasp.

"Easy, Brother. Have no fear of me," she said playfully. "You're among friends."

Percy's face relaxed. "Guess I'm a little on edge, just now. All the excitement. Life in a monastery is supposed to be dull — no excitement at all." He sighed, then smiled.

Elizabeth smiled slyly. "I know about all the excitement going on among the pilgrims. About the German student, I mean." She smirked, folding her arms.

"Oh? Don't be coy, Mademoiselle. Let's have it. Remember? I'm going to leave your papa alone, and you're going to tell me all you hear?"

"No need to be pushy. I'll tell. Papa says he was told by Brother Jean-Baptiste, the Guest House master, that one of the German students has disappeared."

"Yes. That's being gossiped among the monks too."

"The one called Anton. Herr Schmitt. He's gone, they say, and with all his belongings. The old professor and his fellow student say they have no idea where he's gone. The Abbot and Prior checked his room and then went to question the monk who attended the gate last night."

"Did they find him," I asked.

"No. They found the monk at the gate sleeping and learned he'd slept most of the night," she said, leaning in, her eyes narrowing. "He's in big trouble."

She stood up on her crutch and again smiled, like a frog full of flies. Then she walked away, occasionally glancing back and smiling.

"Do you think she knows more than that?" I asked. "Seems to me that she does."

"I don't know what's the matter with her... and... who can tell with someone as devious as that. Maybe. But if so, she'll look for an opportunity to gush and gloat and tell it. Just wait."

As Elizabeth struggled up the pathway, Mr. Westerman — the rich Englishman — came down the path toward us. I didn't much like the look of him — always rubbing his hands and smiling as if he didn't mean it. As he approached, he smiled and said, "Ah, Brother Percy. May I have a word with you?"

"Certainly," said Percy, as the two moved off toward the entrance of the Guest House. I continued my sweeping and learned only much later what was said between them.

"I've been meaning to speak with you for some time, Brother," Mr. Westerman began, smiling nervously. "I'll be brief and to the point." He kept his voice low.

"Yes?"

"I wish to leave an offer with you, m'lad. A generous proposal, you might say. It's about that book, you see. The missing book?"

"Oh?" said Percy, growing suspicious.

"If you can obtain it for me, I will give you £50,000 and a ticket to any-where you choose. Might keep you out of prison, eh? They're saying the German student took it, but I suspect the Abbot and Prior will return their attention to you, eventually."

Percy shuddered and gave a slight gasp. There was a long pause, as Mr. Westerman waited for Percy to reply. However, Percy said nothing.

"Well, then, we know where we stand, eh? You have only to deliver the book, to obtain the reward," the Englishman continued, nodding his head and patting Percy on the shoulder.

"Yes, I see," Percy finally said, as Mr. Westerman smiled and continued on his way.

When Percy returned to the Guest House steps, I asked, "Whatever did Mr. Westerman want?"

Percy looked at me a brief moment. "Oh, he wanted to know if I'd learned more about the German student, but I could tell him nothing, of course."

"Oh."

2

Pilgrims come in all sorts. I have learned that in my years in the monastery and by my work as a servant to those whose faith brings them to Saint Hilda. Some are so sad and turned inward they hardly speak. Others are angry, like the girl, Elizabeth — angry at God maybe, for the burden of their sickness and affliction. Still others are surprisingly happy, just to be in the spiritual climate of the monastery and joyous to be close to our beloved Saint Hilda. Such a one as this last had only been with us a day before Percy and I had occasion to meet her.

Sister Rose's face—surrounded by her habit—was red, flat, and weath-ered, with small, close-set eyes and a large nose. Sister Rose was a frightful sight, except that she had an open, generous smile. Sister Fiona — her young companion — was petite and pretty, and it was said she'd been sent on pilgrimage to assist old Sister Rose, who was too frail to travel alone. Somehow, it made both of them seem special. They had come from Ireland, where our dear Saint Hilda was born.

Percy and I first observed the nuns one morning, as we served the pilgrims at breakfast. They had just arrived, and already Sister Rose was locked in an excited conversation about Saint Hilda with the American, Mr. Covington. Making a fierce point of some kind, she pointed excitedly with the fork in her right hand, while holding Mr. Covington's hand with her left. Percy, I noticed, gazed at Sister Rose with a strange intensity, especially at her weathered hands.

The old nun's smile was catching, and I noticed that everyone she talked to smiled back — even those, like the English ladies, not given to much smiling. And her Irish voice — clear and strong — seemed like sunshine made audible. I had never in my life heard such a voice.

The Irish nuns were the latest of the pilgrims to arrive for the Lenten Season and the last. Prior Oswald told us Sister Rose was suffering from a terrible sickness that would surely take her life, though she might seem healthy, and she had wanted to visit Sister Hilda before she died. Her jovial ways surprised me all the more.

Later that morning, on the path to the Cloister, the old nun took Percy by the elbow and stopped him. I stopped too, a little surprised.

"Brother Percy," she said, her eyes smiling. "I have heard the suspicion about you."

"Oh?" Percy asked, clearly wondering, as I was, what she would make of it.

"I want you to know that I am praying for you, young Brother — praying that God will take this trouble from you and from this holy place. That's the only thing to do, you see. Pray."

"Thank you, Sister," said Percy, as the old nun nodded and continued on her way.

We worked all morning at the Guest House, and later Brother Jean-Baptiste put us to real labor in the garden that surrounds it — more work there than usual, but also more opportunity to observe the pilgrims in their daily routine. I am always encouraged spiritually by the devotion the pilgrims show toward our beloved Saint Hilda.

The pilgrim nuns lingered in the garden a long while, smiling with Father Enrico, I noticed, and it seemed to me they must have become great friends. I observed that the nuns also engaged often with the other pilgrims.

Later, Percy and I were back at our mopping, in the east wing of the Guest House's upper story, where we saw the American, Mr. Covington, descend the stairs.

"That's odd," I heard Percy say to himself.

"What?"

"Mr. Covington. The American."

"Yes. The Americans are odd, indeed. I suppose it's because they associate so much with the wild Indians who...."

"No. Not odd like that," he cut me short.

"What, then?"

"Why was he in the upper-east wing? His room is in the lower-west."

"Oh," I said, wondering why Percy found that remarkable.

"Who resides in that wing?" he asked me. I had to think for a moment. "The English women and Father Enrico," I believe.

He did not reply.

At mid-afternoon, Brother Jean-Baptiste sent us with the monks who each afternoon accompanied the pilgrims to their prayers at the crypt. It was sometimes during these prayers, I was often told, that the miraculous cures had happened, though I had not yet witnessed one during my time at the abbey.

As we moved slowly in our procession down the path, Mr. Covington and Father Enrico came up from the direction of the Precipice. The Precipice is a high cliff, just down from the Cloister, which falls-off sharply into the valley of the Aarn. There, the abbey has made a garden, with stone benches — an excellent place for prayer and contemplation. The two joined our procession. They made a strange pair, and I thought it odd that they should be down there, but the pilgrims sometimes formed friendships during their stays.

About half-way through the devotion, Lady Dorothy suddenly began to cry and quickly commenced to wailing and begging God's forgiveness. At first, I thought we must surely be witnessing a miraculous cure, but then she began to flail about and to cause such a scene that I thought she would overturn her Bath chair. Her nurse, Mrs. Downey, motioned for help to escort the poor girl to the Guest House. I'd never seen such a ruckus at pilgrim prayers before, but the devotion soon continued. As we prayed, I noticed that Mademoiselle Elizabeth, her head bowed, was nonetheless looking sidelong at Percy in the strangest way, but Percy was looking after the English girl, as she was led away. It was then I saw that Mr. Covington, who sat beside M. Dugard, was also looking back, after Lady Dorothy.

3

Once prayers were over and the pilgrims had returned to their House, I could see Percy had fallen into a brooding silence.

"What is it, Percy? Lady Dorothy's strange behavior, eh?"

"No. Just something that may mean nothing."

"What?"

"Let me ask you, Gabriel. Who was not at prayers?"

Now, that just shows you about Percy. Always asking questions no one else thinks about, or even cares about. "I don't know, Percy. I can tell you who was there, but...."

"Then, I'll tell you. Five pilgrims — Dr. Eidenbuch, Herr Becker, Mr. Westerman and the nuns. Hate to sound like a schoolmaster, but I wonder why some were absent, eh?"

"Well, maybe Sister Rose was feeling poorly, but I can't think why the others did not attend."

Percy and I continued up the path, and as we entered the Cloister, I heard a voice behind us. "Wait," she said. We turned together and saw it was Elizabeth, struggling up the path on her crutch. When she reached us, she looked furtively from one side to the other and then whispered, "I hear that Father Abbot and the others are searching about the village for the German student."

"Oh?" I said. "Percy and I have not yet heard that, but I'm not surprised. They must be suspecting it was Herr Schmitt who took the book. Prior Oswald is very keen to get that book."

"No need for searching," said Elizabeth, stiffening her neck. "I told Papa there's a simple explanation. They have only to ask Lady Dorothy."

"The English girl? Who just went berserk?" I asked.

"Yes," she teased.

"Mademoiselle!" said Percy, frowning. "Stop the prattle, and tell us what you know."

"Oh, very well. I suppose I should before you start imagining all sorts of silly things. Especially after that scene, the English lady made at the prayers. You have no sense of suspense, and I shouldn't wonder a boy monk would have no sense of romance either."

"Romance? What about romance?" Percy asked.

"Lady Dorothy and Anton, of course. That's what."

Percy's eyes narrowed, suspiciously, and he gave me a significant glance. "So, you're saying Lady Dorothy and Herr Schmitt are... well...?"

"Yes. They were carrying on. I know it," she said, with a smirk. "At least, I saw them talking more than once, and anyone who has a brain and half an eye for such things as romance could see there's something there," she said, eying Percy with a look that expressed both pity and disappointment.

"Pretty clear to me that Lady Dorothy has rejected Anton and of course the rejected lover has done the most reckless thing he could think of. He has slipped off to who-knows-where in the middle of the night. Never to be seen again. I told Papa to tell the Abbot to question Lady Dorothy and the entire brouhaha will be cleared up," she said, grinning in that self-satisfied way that only a rich, smug, and spoiled French girl with a chip on her shoulder can smile.

"And so, what does this vital information about romance have to do with me? What use is it, when I am trying to figure out what to do about the book? Eh?"

"Nothing. Just something interesting that's happening, on top of everything else, I suppose. I only told you to prevent you from going off on a wild goose chase." And with that Elizabeth turned on her crutch and walked away, shaking her head.

"That girl is a pill," said Percy. "A complete pill and a monumental annoyance. Here I stand, trying to think what to do next, and she comes along gushing tales of romance among the pilgrims."

I agreed with Brother Percy that Elizabeth was indeed strange, but it seemed to me that her information — or rather, her suspicions — might be useful.

Just then, the second bell rang for Vespers. Percy and I looked at each other in fright. We were late. Again. Rushing through the Cloister toward the door to the chapel, there suddenly stepped from the Warming Room another of the pilgrims — the young Italian priest. Father Enrico stumbled forward on his cane and bumped right into Percy, and then fell backward, spilling the books he was carrying as he tumbled to the ground.

"Oh pardon me, Father," Percy begged, as we lifted the poor little priest to his feet. Then Percy fell to one knee and began to gather up the scattered books and the cane. He rose and handed them to Father Enrico, who smiled and repeated, "Oh 'twas nothing. Excuse me, please," he said, as I dusted him. "Excuse me, please." Smiling, as if embarrassed by the disturbance, he moved on toward who knew where.

Percy looked after him a long while, and when he turned back toward me, I could see his face looked oddly puzzled.

"What is it? Do you think he was injured?"

"No, not that."

"What then? I thought we were hurrying to Vespers because we're late."

"Shoes."

"Shoes? What about shoes? Percy, stop muddling about and tell me what 'Shoes' means," I said, with a touch more exasperation than I usually had about Percy, and still fretting that we were late.

"Two things. You've probably noticed how shabby Father Enrico is. His cassock is tattered at the sleeves and a little threadbare elsewhere."

"Yes, but not unusual for a parish priest to be poor. Such men are often the poorest of the poor of their parishes. You said so yourself, about your own father."

"Then why does this poor parish priest wear expensive shoes?"

"What?"

"As I was helping him up, I noticed them. Finely made, and in Milan, I think."

"Milan? Oh, come now."

"Yes. The styling and stitching say they come for Milan. They're distinctive."

"Percy you astonish... but you said there was something else. What?"

"Oh, yes. Something even more interesting. Have you noticed the way Father walked away from us? With each step, he holds the cane in his right hand and drags the interior toe of his left foot."

"No, I just noticed he limps... but if you say so...."

Percy looked at me as if I should have noticed. "The right interior toes of his left shoe should be worn by a walk like that, but it isn't. Not at all."

"Good Heavens! What does that mean?"

"It means the little priest does not often walk that way. That's what it means." Then he smiled his evil smile.

Chapter Six

Wherein 1 Am Almost Eaten

5 April 1911

1

The next day, after our Guest House chores, Percy and I joined several of the other monks who had gathered in the Warming Room, as a frigid north wind blew through the Cloister, fairly chilling my bones.

Brother Paul, an aged German monk, was the only one lolling about the hearth itself, where Percy and I stuck our hands to warm. Being a friendly sort, the old monk asked, "Where have you young brothers come from? Out in the wind, I'll guess."

Percy knew, as I did, that Brother Paul was perhaps the best scholar in the monastery, after the Abbot himself. He was almost always to be found in the Scholarium, studying the ancient manuscripts and making notes from them.

"You know, Brother, that the book is missing. What do you make of that?" Percy asked, in an offhanded way. Still, the old monk seemed a little startled by the directness of Percy's question, but then he smiled. "Oh, I don't know what to think of it. I suppose someone's made off with it, probably hoping to sell it for a bit of ready money. Doubt we shall ever see it again. All the more reason to better safeguard our other manuscripts, I think."

"A sound attitude," I agreed. "Let us be more vigilant."

"Poor Prior Oswald is especially distressed, and I can see why," Brother Paul sighed. "It was his duty to guard the book, and he feels the sting of failure."

"Were you familiar with this book, Brother?" Percy asked, his eyes keen. "You've studied many of the manuscripts, I know. This one too, perhaps?"

Brother Paul nodded agreeably and smiled. "Oh yes. I vaguely recall examining it, years ago. My memory's not what it was, you know...." He smiled, in a vacant sort of way.

"Do you remember anything about the manuscript?"

"Well," he said, looking as if momentarily lost in his thoughts, "...well, I remember it was said to have been brought to the monastery by our beloved Saint Hilda, so it was a very moving experience, as I held something that had been in her own hands. I was moved, I can tell you. There are no other books in our collection that once belonged to a saint, eh? So, there was that."

"What else?" Percy asked quickly.

"Oh yes. The book itself, you mean. Well, I'm not sure I made much of it. Prior Oswald and I discussed the thing because, as I recall, we studied it at the same time."

"So you were able to read it? You and Prior Oswald?"

"Yes. Parts of it. At least, I tried."

"Tried?"

"For one thing, much of it was a jumbled mess of Latin and nonsense words. Even for an early manuscript, there were so many vernacular references — ancient Gaelic, I guessed — that we could not understand, so it was hard to follow. I remember Oswald and I both complained of that. Oswald soon gave it up. Just too many strange words. And then there was the Latin itself. It seemed to be the work of someone poorly schooled in the language."

"It was a mess about what? What was the book about?"

For the first time, Brother Paul seemed uneasy about Percy's questions. "You might say it is a medical book, but not in the usual way," he explained.

"What then?"

"Potions and ointments and such that seemed to me more like magic than science. Even magical incantations and the like, eh?"

"Magic to do what?" Percy asked, leaning in.

"As I say, I could not make much of it, and that's why I too gave it up. But it seemed to be a book of recipes to heal... to cure diseases. Still... I don't know... it all just seemed such a jumble to me. And it was long ago, so I remember even less," he sighed. "What would our beloved Saint Hilda want with such a book?" He shook his head.

Percy fell silent, with a look on his face that told me he'd heard much less than he'd hoped.

"It's bitter cold this Lent, I must say," Brother Paul complained, in his dreamy way, changing the subject.

Percy looked at him in a sidelong way and smiled. "Oh yes, Brother. A chilly season for sure."

"Must be off to prepare for Sext (noon). We shall soon hear the bell for the mid-day prayers, I think," said the old brother.

As Percy watched him shuffle toward the door, he said, "Gabriel, did it seem to you Brother Paul was not saying all he knows? Or, am I just too suspicious?"

"I hesitate to answer about one as saintly as Brother Paul, but yes, Percy. It seemed to me he held back. I sensed it, especially at the end. But then, he told us he found the book disturbing. Anyway, Percy, I'm not sure Brother Paul's mind is quite right these days. He's old and forgetful and just a little unsteady, if you ask me."

"Ask Timothy what he thinks."

Without my asking, Timothy whispered immediately into my mind, "He was holding back." I conveyed that to Percy, who smiled. "That Timothy's got a head on his shoulders if angels actually have shoulders."

"That Percy is one smart sinner. He's asking all the right questions, and he's making all the right conclusions about the answers he's getting," Timothy replied into my mind. "He might just figure this thing out if he lives long enough."

I expected Percy to tell me more of what he was suspecting, but he said nothing. We continued to warm when suddenly we heard shouts and screaming from outside — in the Cloister. Percy looked up at me, then we both sprang for the door.

Just beyond the door, we found Elizabeth, staring across the Cloister, shaking, her face rigid with fear. I looked where she was looking, and out of the corner of my eye, I saw the fleeting shadow of something. At first, I was confused by all the ruckus, but then I saw it.

2

On the far side of the Cloister, not ten meters from us, there stood a large black wolf. His back turned to us, his attention fixed on Lady Dorothy and her nurse, Mrs. Downey, their escape blocked by a hedge on one side and the wolf on the other. They cowered, clearly afraid that any attempt to run would bring the snarling creature upon them. When the wolf heard us, he turned and looked at me, lowing like a cow, moving his head from side to side, his eyes fierce, his mouth frothing and dripping saliva.

When the beast turned, Percy snatched Elizabeth's crutch and ran into the center of the Cloister, where there stands a statue of St. Benedict, upon a pedestal. Keeping the pedestal between him and the wolf, Percy began to taunt the animal, clearly wanting to distract it from the women. He succeeded. It began to snarl at Percy and moved cautiously toward him and the pedestal, growling. Just then, Percy managed to catch the wolf a blow on the head with the crutch, as he ran to one side and the other of the pedestal, doing his best to confuse the rabid creature.

The wolf grew angrier, and worse still, Lady Dorothy and Mrs. Downey made no effort to escape, as Percy clearly hoped they would. I shouted to them, "Run! Get away while Percy distracts the wolf." But no use. They remained frozen in fear, only now for some reason, they both decided to start screaming, like a pair of lost souls.

Percy continued his frenzied dance around the pedestal, relying on good St. Benedict to protect him, taunting and confusing the wolf, whose eyes flashed with rage. At one point, the beast lunged so quickly that he almost caught Percy's arm, but Percy was quick, and as the wolf missed, he gave him another cracking blow to the back of the head. Still, I began to wonder how long Percy could keep up the game before the wolf would get lucky.

At the same time, as I was cowering, perspiring, chewing my lower lip, and trying to get up my courage, Elizabeth hobbled into the center of the Cloister, shouting and waving her arms like a lunatic, dragging her bad foot behind her, trying desperately to gain the wolf's attention. To my fright, she was successful. He turned on her, just as she stumbled forward and fell. I ran after her.

Thinking Elizabeth was an easy meal, the wolf lunged at her, but just then Percy sprang forward and gave it another vicious blow to the head, knocking it back. Percy fell to Elizabeth's side to help her to her feet, just as I reached her, and just as the wolf recovered and began to snarl at the three of us. My blood turned cold. He was looking at me.

Then something from another world happened — something that later no one else had apparently noticed. As the wolf flashed his fierce red eyes at me, he spoke to me in a clear, dark voice. "You cannot defeat me, monk. I will have my victory." The wolf was not a wolf at all, but a demon.

As soon as he had spoken his warning, the creature turned once more to Percy, and just as I figured he would soon have one of us in his teeth, I heard a booming sound. Just as suddenly, the wolf dropped to the ground in a heap. For a moment, one of his red eyes fixed on me, but then it faded to darkness. A deathly silence fell over the Cloister. At first, I thought my prayers had brought down God's vengeance on the terrible creature, but when I looked around, I saw the American — Mr. Lucas Covington — standing beside Sister Rose, a big, smoking pistol in his hand.

3

I don't know why things pop into my head at the oddest times, but my immediate thought was that one is not supposed to have a whacking big pistol in the monastery. But then, I remembered that Mr. Covington is an American, and those people are prone to do the oddest things, like going about the Cloister with a whacking big pistol. Suddenly, I was happy that Americans are odd in certain ways.

I turned to look at Percy — panting, exhausted, leaning against the pedestal, holding Elizabeth in his arms and still gripping her crutch. Now, the Cloister filled with shouting monks and pilgrims, including Father Abbot and Prior Oswald. Mr. Covington advanced on the wolf cautiously, pointing his pistol as he did so. Monsieur Dugard arrived and ran to Elizabeth's side.

"Thank God you were able to intervene, Mr. Covington!" said Dugard.

"Praise God for your quick thinking," exclaimed Father Abbot, his face ashen, his eyes anguished.

The American smirked, as he tucked the pistol inside his coat. "I got here late, Father Abbot. Almost too late. It was those two who distracted the wolf from killing someone," he said, nodding toward Percy and Elizabeth.

Father Abbot looked toward Percy, who was now sitting on the ground, his back resting against good St. Benedict's pedestal and still holding Elizabeth's hand. "Yes," said Sister Rose, enthusiastically, as she took Elizabeth in her arms. "Brother Percy attacked the wolf. With Elizabeth's crutch, you see, and then this brave girl went to his aid. As did Brother Gabriel."

Percy righted himself and faced Elizabeth. "Your crutch, Mademoiselle. Thank you for the loan." He smiled, bowing slightly.

"Well," said Prior Oswald. "A tragedy has been averted, and we may thank you, Mr. Covington, and of course Brother Percy here, also. Yes. Thanks to God, and to the both of you." It seemed odd to me that even as he was thanking Percy, Brother Prior managed to look down his nose and sniff disapproval.

"And now," Father Abbot added, "if Brother Percy and Brother Gabriel will drag the wolf's carcass over to Precipice and throw him over, we will all return to our duties. Brother Prior, will you see to the Lady Dorothy and Mrs. Downey? Thank you."

While Percy and I struggled to drag the giant wolf's body toward the Precipice the crowd dispersed. All except Elizabeth and her parents, that is. She remained and for some reason continued to look at Percy for the longest while.

Chapter Seven
Wherein A Tragedy
Changes Everything

6-7 April 1911

1

The excitement of a raging wolf fades slowly in the dull routine of a monastery. Everyone remained on edged the entire day that followed. I told no one — not even Percy — that the creature had spoken to me. Still, more than one of the monks that day told me the wolf was a demon and perhaps even one of those imps known to invade monasteries from time to time. Brother Jean-Baptiste called the wolf a dreadful premonition. Some even connected the wolf with the missing book — evil would come upon the abbey as long as the relic remained missing, they warned. Brother Félix, a usually jovial old French monk, said the wolf was surely a visitation by Satan himself, probably jealous of the abbey's joy at the coming Resurrection of Our Lord. Many of the brothers agreed and whispered prayers. The monks, you see, believe that Satan is especially eager to do his mischief in places of holy reflection and prayer; such is his hatred of God.

After battling the wolf, Percy seemed quieter and more thoughtful. Elizabeth was silent and not angry — both unusual for her — and the pilgrims mumbled to each other. The experience made me wonder at Percy's courage to attack the wolf, and at his legwork, as he ran around the saint's pedestal, this way and that, to confuse it. And then I thought about Mr. Covington and his large American pistol. I still continued to worry that someone would bring such a thing into our monastery.

That morning, as the monks emerged from Lauds, I found Percy wearing a dazed look on his face.

"What?" I asked.

"The French girl," he said, without looking at me. "She risked her life to save me. *Quelle courage!*"

"Yes. I remember how bravely she staggered out to help you. That girl has plenty of grit. Maybe it's something about being French?"

"No, it's something about being Elizabeth," he said.

Percy had the last word on Elizabeth's bravery, as the bell rang silence for breakfast.

It was market day for the people of Chaumont, who gathered early in the forecourt. On market days, Prior Oswald assigned Percy and me to visit each vendor and beg the customary donation for the monastery. Percy is really good at begging, putting the most pitiful expression in his voice. The pilgrims were also free to visit the market and to buy what provisions they wished. I enjoyed the market because it gave me a glimpse of the lives of vendors from the town. Very interesting to see and to talk to them.

Early on, Percy and I encountered Mr. Covington, who accompanied the little Italian priest, Father Enrico. I was pleased that Father Enrico greeted us in a cheerful way, after his painful collision with Percy. No hard feelings, I supposed. Then, we noticed Elizabeth and her parents, out early in the market, looking at this and that. When Elizabeth spied us, she followed Percy with her eyes.

"Good Morning, to ye," said a cheerful voice. "A beautiful day the Lord has made, eh?" said Sister Rose, in her happy way.

"Nice work, young Brother," she patted Percy on the shoulder. "Your dancin' about with the wolf saved Lady Dorothy, I have no doubt. You did well of yourself, Brother Percy." She smiled and nodded.

Percy merely smiled in return.

"Ah the wolves are indeed strange creatures, but let's not believe the nonsense the monks are sayin' about Satan visitin' the abbey, eh?"

"Then you have some familiarity with wolves, Sister?" Percy asked.

"Aye, but not since I was a girl on m'father's farm, God rest him. Sure they're a curse upon Ireland's sheepmen, as elsewhere, they are."

"Not so much for the Swiss," said Percy, "but I'm told they sometimes cause trouble. Never a care, Sister. Brother Gabriel and I do not accept the business about Satan."

I was not so sure, myself.

"Wolves will be wolves, and those that come down with the frothing sickness will be a trouble, sooner or later," I added, as the happy nun and Sister Fiona turned and strolled away. I imagined that Sister Rose spoke much as our beloved Saint Hilda might have spoken, with that musical lilt in her voice. After all, she too was Irish — and a nun.

Just then — I don't know why — I caught sight of Mr. Westerman, who was looking our way. Percy saw him too, and returned his glance, but said nothing. What was that about, I wondered?

Percy and I lingered in the market all day and finished our collections just as the bell rang for Vespers. As we scurried toward the chapel, Percy asked me an odd question.

"Why does Father Enrico always speak to us in French? I am English and you are German-speaking Swiss. The monks here all speak Latin to one another. Why not Latin?"

"I don't know. I can see his French is good, though with a noticeable accent." I thought for a moment. "Perhaps his Latin is not as good as his French, or perhaps he just prefers it. I don't begrudge him his preference. Don't much like to speak Latin, myself. It's just too complicated as talking goes. You have to think too much when you speak it. Mr. Covington's pistol, for example. I had an awful time yesterday, trying to figure out how to say a pistol in Latin. There's no word for it."

"Yes," said Percy. "I know what you mean. Still, we must make a point of speaking Latin to Father Enrico."

I started to ask why, but just then we reached the chapel, where the brothers were already assembled for prayer. As we took our seats Father Abbot looked at us down his long nose to where his little spectacles perched. Prior Oswald, who sat beside him, gave Percy his usual menacing scowl and then sniffed.

In the spring, the sun begins to sink beyond the high mountains later and the alpine dusk always seems to have a special hue of blue and purple. I was thinking how beautiful it was, as we emerged from prayers and crossed the Cloister to the Refectory. It was then — in the beautiful evening gleam — we heard the heart-stopping scream.

2

The sound had come from the north — just beyond the hedge that lined the Cloister. From the direction of the Precipice. I feared that someone — one of the pilgrims, maybe — had stumbled over in the dim light of dusk.

The monks ran toward the Precipice, led by Prior Oswald. I started after them and would have been out front in no time, except that Percy took my forearm.

"Hold back, Brother," he said, as we watched the old monks and Father Abbot at the rear of the crowd scrambling toward the Precipice. By the time we caught up, the brothers were mumbling among themselves about what one could see below. There, not two meters from the carcass of the wolf and forty meters below us, lay a body, face down, so we could not make him out — not from that distance, anyway.

"Brother Johann," Father Abbot ordered. "Get ropes, and go down there to see to that man."

Johann -- one of the lay-brothers — is the most experienced mountaineer among us. He returned shortly, and as eight or ten of us held the rope, he lowered himself down the steep face of the Precipice, until he'd reached the body. By now, most of the pilgrims had joined us, as we all gawked and waited.

"He's dead, sure enough," Johann shouted up, to no one's surprise. We watched as Johann fixed his end of the rope around the corpse and made a kind of halter.

"Hoist him," said Johann, waving his arms.

We began to pull on the rope — hand-over-hand — one measured tug after another. It seemed the longest time that we pulled, though the weight at the end did not seem so great. Finally, we dragged a body over the edge of the Precipice, his back still turned toward us. Prior Oswald fell to one knee and turned him over. "Father Enrico!" someone shouted in disbelief. We all gasped and crossed ourselves.

The monks and pilgrims murmured even louder, to think that a priest had died. Father Abbot led us in The Lord's Prayer, over the body. "We'll not be talking Latin to Father Enrico," I whispered to Percy. "Except in our prayers for him, of course."

"Lower the rope to Brother Johann," Prior Oswald ordered. When Johann came over the Precipice I noticed he had with him a rucksack. "The Father had this with him, so I thought to bring it up," he said, handing it to Father Abbot.

By this time, Elizabeth stood beside us, and next to her, her parents. I noticed also she had taken hold of Percy's forearm. We gazed — disbelieving — upon the dead priest's body. Father Abbot and Prior Oswald opened the rucksack, and as they looked in, their jaws dropped in unison.

"What is it?" Monsieur Dugard asked. Father Abbot stood speechless for a long moment. Then, he took from the rucksack the last thing I had expected to see. It was an old book, and I knew at once it must be the book. The missing book. Prior Oswald opened it, as those of us nearby leaned in, and we could see it was indeed an ancient manuscript.

"Yes!" he exclaimed. "It is... this is it... Saint Hilda's book!"

The monks and pilgrims all fell to loud murmuring. Father Abbot reached once more into the rucksack and drew out a large wallet, brimming with money. Almost overflowing with bank notes — "French francs from the look of it," Percy whispered in my ear, "and lots of 'em." Father Enrico had stolen the book and was making off with it and a substantial sum of money — maybe money he'd been paid to steal our book.

"That's exactly what I was thinking," Timothy whispered into my mind.

I looked at Percy. For some reason, he was looking at Monsieur Dugard, who had taken the book from Prior Oswald and was glancing through its pages. I noticed Percy stretching his neck to see the pages too, as Monsieur Dugard turned them, and then paused to examine one more closely.

In the next instant, I saw that Mr. Westerman was standing beside Monsieur Dugard, looking at the book and then at Percy, and Percy was looking at him.

It seemed that Father Abbot took a minute or two to settle his emotions. "We must summon the canton police," he declared. "Prior Oswald, please see to that." Father Abbot then ordered some of the monks to carry Father Enrico's body to the Brew House, a cold place where the dead of our monastery were customarily prepared for burial.

3

Percy and I joined those who carried the body, and when we had placed Father Enrico on a table, Percy said we must search his pockets for anything that might help the police determine what had happened. The brothers agreed, but we found nothing, which Percy seemed to find interesting. When we emerged once more into the Cloister, Percy took me aside.

"Did you notice the look on Monsieur Dugard's face when he examined the book?"

"Yes. He looked surprised. We all were surprised to find it, and I am delighted. The monks are whispering that Father Enrico must have taken the book, and so now you are relieved of suspicion entirely, Percy. I am happy for you."

"Yes, that's at least one thing, but there's much more to the priest's death. Or, rather, his murder."

"Murder?" I gasped. "Surely not. He was out to the Precipice and lost his footing. That must be what happened. A mishap."

"Before we argue that point, let's be off to the Guest House, to have a look at his room," said Percy. "We might find something interesting there."

Percy was right. When we looked into Father Enrico's room, we found what looked to be all of his belongings. If the rucksack meant he was intending to travel, why had he left so much behind?

Percy gazed intently at all the things we'd collected and laid out on the bed. "Gabriel, do you notice what's not here?"

Now, there you see it again, I told myself. Percy is forever asking questions about things ordinary people don't think to ask.

The question puzzled me, so I looked more closely. Soon, my head began to ache. "No," I confessed. "What?"

"There's nothing here a priest would be expected to have — no bible, rosary, prayer book — nothing of that sort. And why would he leave his watch behind?" asked Percy, as he picked up a gold watch and chain from the table beside the Father's bed.

"What do you make of that, then?" I asked, as confused as ever at what Percy was suggesting.

"I do not believe Father Enrico was planning to travel at all, and I doubt he was a priest. That's what. He went out to the Precipice to meet someone, who already had the rucksack. That person pushed Father Enrico over and tossed the rucksack after him."

"With the book? And money? But why throw away the book? And, the money? If that murderer was the person who stole the book, why throw it away? That's nonsense, Percy."

"Maybe for the same reason that Monsieur Dugard was frowning," he replied. Before I could ask what he meant by that, he dashed for the walkway that leads from the Guest House to the Cloister.

"Where are we off to now?" I asked, running to keep up with him.

"The Dugards were in the Refectory when we left. If they're still there, I would very much like to have a word in private with Elizabeth's papa."

"Why?"

"Because I think he knows what I know about that book."

"What's that?"

Chapter Eight
Wherein Monsieur Dugard
Tells What He Knows

8 April 1911

1

We did not find the Dugards after all, until the next morning when we met them on the path to the saint's tomb. They were bound for pilgrim prayers.

"Monsieur Dugard. Bonjour, Monsieur," Percy hailed, as the three stopped and waited for us to approach.

Monsieur Dugard was a tall, handsome man -- slender, with a balding head, and neatly trimmed grey beard, and what they call an aristocratic nose. He always carried a cane, though he did not need assistance in walking, and he wore a stylish hat, like the English King. Despite his middle years, he walked like a vigorous man. Madame Dugard was short and stout — one of those people God intended for endurance rather than speed.

"*Oui*. What is it?" Monsieur Dugard asked, a little impatient at being stopped.

"A word, *s'il vous plaît*," said Percy, smiling and extending his hand. Monsieur Dugard shook it, as Elizabeth and her mama looked-on.

"Of course, but about what? And we are rather in a hurry... for prayers, you see."

"The book we saw," Percy replied, his eyes narrowing and his voice falling to a whisper.

"*Oui*," he said, startled as if he did not much like being asked about the book. "The book? The book in the rucksack, you mean? The one that was missing but is now recovered."

"Precisely," Percy replied. "The very one. I noticed you took a great interest in it. Of course, as everyone knows, I have been suspected of stealing the thing."

"But now you are proved innocent," said Elizabeth, smiling broadly.

"Yes. That's one thing," Percy agreed, "but then there is the book, which was indeed taken."

"By Father Enrico," said Dugard.

"Yes... it was certainly found with his body," Percy agreed. "No one would dispute that. Still, it's not where or how it was found that interests me just now. It's the book itself. Forgive me, but I noticed the surprised expression on your face as you examined it, Monsieur, and I wondered what that was all about."

Dugard stiffened and raised his chin, then looked down at Percy with a forceful eye. He was thinking, but about what? "You are observant, Brother Percy," he finally replied, giving Percy a slightly suspicious look.

"I try Monsieur. I've had to learn to be aware of things. It can save one's life, you know. From time to time."

Again, Dugard lapsed into a thoughtful silence. "Well, yes. I was eager to see the book because such things are my business. I am a dealer in rare books, eh? I had heard of the theft and given the chance to see the book itself... well, I was interested. Very interested."

"And what did you observe?" Percy probed, leaning in.

"Very well, Brother Percy. You are pursuing me like you chased that wolf. You wish to know what I know about that book, eh?"

"No. I wish to know if you know the same thing that I know about it."

Monsieur Dugard raised both eyebrows, then smiled faintly. "Then perhaps you will tell me, and I will agree or disagree, Brother Percy."

2

"The history of the book, as I understand it," Percy began, "is that it was brought to the abbey by Saint Hilda, who we know died in 1134. She had fled Ireland and later Normandy because of all the war going on between King Stephen and the Empress Maude. She came here and brought the book with her, they say."

"Yes, that is so," I said. "She died and left the book. Father Abbot says so."

Percy looked at Monsieur Dugard. "The book we saw could not have been written before 1134 and that is a problem, is it not, Monsieur?"

Dugard smiled again. "Please continue, Brother Percy."

"Gladly. It's the script," said Percy. "It's all wrong. It's a variation of the script that Saint Hilda's book would have been written in, but it is a later variation."

"What!" I exclaimed. "You lost me, I'm afraid."

"Me too," said Elizabeth. But Monsieur Dugard merely smiled more broadly.

Percy explained further, still peering into Monsieur Dugard's eyes. "The prevailing script of the time — known as the Caroline Minuscule* — emerged to become the standard in the second half of the tenth century. That's the script that prevailed up to the time of Saint Hilda's death. However, the book we saw was written in a later variation of the Caroline Minuscule — a style that's known today as the German Protogothic Bookhand, and which only emerged in the second half of the twelfth century — well after Saint Hilda was already in her crypt Is that not so, Monsieur?"

Dugard's face suddenly flashed excitement, like a man who could hardly contain his joy. "You have explained it, precisely, Brother Percy, and you amaze me that you should know. You have a keen eye and an expert's knowledge. Only a true expert in such things would know that," he said, smiling his admiration and shaking Percy's hand vigorously.

"It's my business to know such things, rather like it is yours, Monsieur Dugard. But the point now is...."

"Yes. The point is, if that book could not have belonged to Saint Hilda, where did it come from, eh?" Dugard asked. "I have wondered over that one myself. And, I have concluded there are two possible answers. The first is that the entire business about the book is a fabrication and the book in the monastery is a fraud. I have encountered such things in my business."

"And the second?" Percy asked, as his eyes narrowed.

"Ah, that's a much more delicious possibility," said Dugard, smiling.

Percy smiled too, which told me he had thought of the same thing.

"That the book in the abbey is a copy of an older book, which was lost, perhaps?"

"Exactly," Percy said. "And perhaps not a very good copy at that. But it is written in the German Protogothic Bookhand, which was the very script used in this monastery after the middle of the twelfth century, and that leads me to think the book we've all seen was made right here."

"Well, Brother Percy, you have seen all that is possible to see in that book, and you are suspecting all the right things. But only God knows what is true, I think," Dugard shrugged.

Percy's face continued grim. "One other thing, Monsieur, if you please?"

"Certainly," said Dugard.

"I had never heard of the book — *The Chronicle of Secrets* — before it went missing. Tell me, what do people in your business — bookmen — say about it? Know about it?"

Dugard smiled. "Ah, there you have asked another excellent question. Not much is known at all. Some have whispered about it, here and there, for years, but nothing at all is known. Just rumors."

"What is whispered, then?"

"Some have said it is a complete myth. Others have said it is to be found here, in this monastery, while others claim it is in the Vatican archives. That it is the rarest of all books and...." He paused, clearly to find just the right words "...and it is said to convey miraculous cures. But, Brother Percy, as you know, the book we saw cannot be that book."

"Yes. Probably, but if it's all the same, I think I want to get a closer look at the book found with Father Enrico. The trouble is that neither Father Abbot nor the Prior is likely to allow that. Neither of them trusts me, you see."

"I cannot help you there, young Percy. I asked the Prior if I might examine it more closely, and he refused me. But, good luck," he smiled, as the Dugards turned and continued on their way to join the other pilgrims at the crypt. Five paces down the walk, Elizabeth looked back and smiled.

As we looked after the Dugards, a sudden wind blew in from the high mountains, stirring the trees and bringing with it an unexpected cover of clouds. Dark clouds, of the kind that usually foretell an approaching storm. I pulled up the cowl of my robe around my ears.

Percy had already turned and was making his way up the path toward the Cloister. And no wonder his rush. The bell was ringing for Terce (9 a.m.), and we were sure to be late once again.

3

The prayers proceeded as usual and without event. I sometimes glanced toward Father Abbot, as we chanted our prayers, and I could see his face, riven with the pain of recent events. As we finished, he stood.

"Brothers," he began, his voice weaker than usual, "Great tragedy has come upon our community. We are under attack by The Evil One, I feel it. His menace hangs over our beloved abbey, and as we all know, the answer to such things is faith and prayer. So, I am declaring three days of perpetual prayer. Two brothers will pray here in the church constantly, for four hour periods, except when we are all in prayer."

This only fueled the talk of demons and evil forces. Now, it was even being whispered by some, we learned, that one of Satan's lieutenants — a demon — was living among us. "An evil entity," said Brother Felix, "named Moloch, who has taken the form of one of the pilgrims, or even one of the brothers." I crossed myself just to think it, though I could not imagine how Brother Felix knew the demon by his name.

Prior Oswald soon posted a schedule for prayer. It assigned Brother Percy and me the hours next morning before Matins (2:30-3:00 a.m.). As was the custom in times of vigils and perpetual prayer, two brother monks prayed together, so that each could keep the other awake.

Later, we also learned from Prior Oswald that the Abbot had sent for Captain Ulrich, the police prefect of the canton. He would arrive the next day, it was said.

Chapter Nine
Wherein I Become a Champion Liar

9 April 1911

1

Percy and I prayed our vigil in the eerie silence of the Church. From outside, there came a distant rumble of thunder, and inside, the only light shone from the flickering candles on the high altar. Still, even by that dim light, I could see Percy's face. As I prayed my vigil, I was not quite sure what he was thinking, though I knew he was not sleeping. I suspected he was thinking about the book and what we had learned of Father Enrico.

Why does he still care so much about that book, I wondered. It is now returned and he is free of suspicion. In my darkest thoughts, I admit now, I wondered if Percy — the sinful thief — might not be thinking of stealing it. I would have been even more worried if I had known at that time that Mr. Westerman had offered him so much money for the book.

Long into our vigil, as my mind began to wander from my prayers, I heard the faintest noise behind me, as if someone, or something, were there. I turned quickly and thought I caught a fleeting impression of someone moving in the shadows.

I turned to see if Percy had noticed it. Apparently not.

Then it began. Softly. The chorus of hellish voices I had heard before. A low, droning chant.

"Do you hear it, Percy?" I whispered.

"What?" he started.

"The voices. The chant."

He looked at me, confused. Then I noticed the voices had gone. "Never mind," I said. "My imagination, I guess."

He smiled.

Next morning, after Lauds, Percy eagerly followed Brother Paul to the Locutory, where monks gathered before breakfast. We took seats on the bench beside him, and, as we awaited the bell to breakfast, Percy asked the old brother his opinion of things.

"I cannot say, but it's all sad." The old monk shook his head. "Very sad that such a death should come into the monastery... poor Father Enrico. I cannot imagine what happened to him."

"The monks say there's a demon amongst us," I suggested. He smiled at me and lowered his head.

"Brother," Percy said very earnestly, "Father Enrico's sad death leads me to want to know more about the book that was found in his rucksack. Aside from Prior Oswald, you are the only monk who has studied the book. It is said you know most about it."

Brother Paul nodded agreeably. "What more do you wish to know, Brother Percy?" he finally asked, apparently resigned to answering more of Percy's questions.

"I'm not sure," Percy explained, "but I wish to know if you know more than you have told."

The old monk looked down at his folded hands and thought for a moment. "Yes," he said, looking up. "There is one thing. I remembered it after we spoke the other day. I don't remember things as well as I once did, you know." He shrugged.

"Oh?" Percy perked up.

"Yes, well... long ago, when last I studied the book... well, aside from all the strange words in it... the book was incomplete."

"What?"

"I followed it to the very end, you see, and I could read it well enough to know that it just stops. Abruptly. No reason why. Just stops." He shook his head and then smiled. "Well, to tell the truth, by that time I was so confused by the gibberish in the book I was convinced it had almost nothing to say, except some strange incantations about healing. So, I did not care much that it ended." He smiled and shrugged. "Well, except for one thing. It troubled me that Saint Hilda should set great store by such a mess. I mean to say, how was it that such a book should be so important to our beloved Saint? That is troubling, is it not?"

"Yes," Percy answered, "but the fact that the book is incomplete — now there's an interesting thing." We continued to sit and wait for the call to breakfast. Soon, however, Brother Paul's face lighted. "There is one other thing, Brother Percy. Now that you ask. I've just thought of it...." He smiled.

"Oh? What?"

"There is Brother Albertus, of course. Have you heard of him?"

"Yes. Not much, but I know he's now a hermit."

"Exactly. Many years ago, we were monks together. Both German. We'd both been to university, and so we shared the same experiences. Most of the monks here are simple Swiss boys — unread, and with little scholarship, you know. Oswald is one of them. Oh, he tried to make something of the book, but he has no scholarship for such things. But, Albertus was different... a brilliant man... well-read... learned... a true scholar. I learned much from him, and I admired him. Oh, yes — fond memories of him." The old monk smiled dreamily and then seemed to drift off.

"Yes?" Percy prompted.

"Well... Albertus, you see... he studied the book as well, now I come to recall it. In fact, as I remember, he claimed to have gleaned a good bit more than I from it, eh? And, it was soon after that Albertus asked to be released from the Cloister to become a hermit. You know, I have always suspected that the book, and what Albertus claimed to know of it, had something to do with his departure." He shook his head.

This sent Percy into a long silence. "What are you thinking, Percy?" I finally asked. No answer. So, I repeated. "What are you thinking?"

Just then the first bell rang, and Brother Paul doddered off to the Refectory, while Percy continued to brood. I asked again, "What are you thinking, Percy?"

"Let Percy think," Timothy scolded. "He's a thinker and a plotter, Gabriel — unlike you."

"Now that you're here, Timothy, what do you know of Albertus?" I dared to ask.

He paused. "There's great danger in the name for you, Gabriel. Beware of Albertus, the hermit. Beware."

To hear that word again — 'Beware' — frightened me.

Later, at Terce, I noticed Prior Oswald eying Percy. While we chanted and prayed, I too sometimes glanced at Percy out of the corner of my eye, and I could see that although he was mouthing the words, he was distracted. I knew the cause. He did not yet know what to do about all he'd learned. I was distressed that he so easily pushed aside my suggestion that he should be content the book was found and happy that he was no longer suspected. Let things go and enjoy his freedom from suspicion.

When I put this to him again after prayers, he explained, "No, Gabriel. There's something very big happening here — something that endangers all of us. Father Enrico didn't die by accident. If he had a partner in stealing the book, who killed him to keep him quiet, why would that person let the book go over the Precipice with him?"

"Maybe the partner made a mistake, and the rucksack got away?"

"Yes, I've considered that too, and in that case, we must ask if the book is still in danger. And, what if Father Enrico was an innocent person, who was merely used by the real thief to throw-off suspicion?"

"No way is the book going to be stolen again. Prior Oswald... well, you know he has hidden it where no thief shall ever find it."

Percy looked at me in his disappointed way, and then said, "Gabriel, you give Prior Oswald far too much credit."

"Amen," I heard Timothy say. "Amongst the guardian angels, Oswald is a well-known dunderhead. Percy's on the ball."

2

The time between Terce and Sext at mid-day is always busy. That day, Percy and I helped in the Refectory, where food was prepared. We often carried meals to the dining room at the Guest House, where the pilgrims always dined separately from the monks and lay-brothers. Often, we stayed and served the pilgrims. As we worked, I lamented that the monastery remained in turmoil because of Father Enrico's death and now with the expected arrival of the chief of the cantonal police, Captain Ulrich. I wondered if he would question every-one or make an arrest, perhaps. And sure enough, as Elizabeth had predicted, there was a flurry of chatter about the German student's disappearance, which only added to the turbulence of things. Had Herr Schmitt killed Father Enrico? And run away? Or, was he dead too? Some of the brothers whispered that both Father Enrico and the German student had been killed by demons, who had come out of the Forest of Ohme to avenge the demon wolf's death. Some even said Herr Schmitt was a demon, who did his evil work and then disappeared.

That set me to thinking deeply, as I sometimes do while I work. Who is the demon? The one Brother Felix called Moloch, I wondered? Someone among the pilgrims? Maybe Mr. Covington — the man with the evil-looking pistol? Ah, someone you'd least suspect, like Madame Dugard or young Sister Fiona?

All this thinking left me confused, except that now I was pretty sure there was indeed a servant of Satan at work in the monastery — poised to strike again. I remembered the frightening chorus of evil voices I'd heard. I shuddered. Then, I heard Timothy shudder, and when guardian angels shudder, the ground around your feet trembles a little.

At the midday meal, I heard Sister Rose express an even stranger notion. "The Saint has spoken it into my mind," she told Madame Dugard. "Father Enrico was no priest a'tall. The Saint feels such a comfort in telling me these things, because I'm an Irish nun like her, and I understand her Gaelic, mind you."

"Has she told you more?" Madame Dugard asked, her eyes wide.

"Oh yes. A good deal more. Father Enrico was making away with his book and the money he'd been paid to steal it when he slipped over the Precipice. That's what the police will find, I assure you, my dear. The Saint says so."

I sighed. Could it be the Saint is talking to Sister Rose, the way Timothy talks to me? I asked myself.

After we had served the mid-day meal at the Guest House, Percy and I found Elizabeth just outside, on the path to the Cloister. She walked with us, but when we'd almost reached our destination, Percy stopped dead in his tracks.

"What is it?" I asked, looking around to see what was the matter.

"It's come to me what I must do now... and how I might do it, but I must have help — from both of you. Are you willing?" he asked, looking from one to the other of us.

"Help with what?" Elizabeth asked.

"Help me get a look at that book, that's what."

She smiled. "Of course."

Meanwhile, I was startled and frightened by Percy's reckless scheming, and even more by Elizabeth's easy way of falling-in with his sneaky ways.

While I had learned to expect nothing but one crazy idea after another from Percy, I'd given Elizabeth more credit for good sense.

Still, I decided at least to listen to Percy's insanity before I objected to it. I heard Timothy say, "Oh my! This is going to be a doozie." I had never heard the word 'doozie' before, and so I supposed it is one of those special angel words that Timothy sometimes uses, but I understood the meaning.

"Listen, Gabriel. I must have a bit of time alone with that book, and we all know that neither Father Abbott nor Brother Oswald is likely to allow it. At the very least, they are keen to kill anything to do with the book and let things die down. Oswald wouldn't even allow Elizabeth's father to have a look at the book, remember?"

"Right." Elizabeth nodded, just as I was thinking it all sounded like a really bad idea.

"Why do you want to be alone with the book, Percy?" I wondered aloud.

"I know it's a long shot, but I want to see for myself what it's about and if I can learn anything about its abrupt ending."

At that moment, Timothy whispered into my mind — "Let Percy do it."

"Fair enough," I said, "but how do you know where the book is kept? After all, Oswald has taken it in charge. And how will you get yourself to it, even if you find where it is?"

Percy looked at me with a slightly impatient squint. "Not absolutely sure where it is, but I can guess. Oswald is a dull fellow if you'll pardon my saying so, and now he's been shaken in his confidence. Where do you suppose he will keep it?"

I had no idea, but Elizabeth spoke up right away. "Under his mattress, of course, where all dullards hide things." She smirked.

Percy smiled. "Exactly. Give the French girl a prize for hitting the bull's eye." Elizabeth smiled.

"That means I must break into Oswald's cell. Once there, I'll need as much time as I can get to find the book and look it over. An hour if possible."

"Good Heavens, Percy! That's a long while," I said. "And this business about breaking into Prior Oswald's...."

"Yes. But I know how to make it happen. That's where you two come in."

We both leaned in. "When Captain Ulrich arrives, Father Abbott and Oswald will be preoccupied with him. They'll latch onto him and not leave his side the entire while."

"Yes, that's true," I agreed.

"That'll be my chance to invade Oswald's cell. And, I have a plan."

I wasn't surprised. Percy is one of those people who always has a plan.

"What is it?" Elizabeth asked, her eyes wide and eager.

"Oswald's cell is at the far end of the Dorter, next to the Father Abbot's rooms. Gabriel, I want you to take up a position at the other end of the Dorter, just at the top of the nightstairs. Elizabeth, you will loiter at the foot of the nightstairs, and if you see Oswald approaching and it appears he is bound for his cell, whistle up the nightstairs to Gabriel. Can you whistle?"

"Of course," she said, insulted that Percy would even ask. She put both index fingers in her mouth and let out a screeching noise.

"Ouch!" I heard Timothy scream in my ear. "Angel ears can't stand whistles! Never do that, if you want to keep your guardian angel around." I looked to my left and saw Timothy on the ground, dazed and still holding his ears.

"That will be your signal, Gabriel."

"My signal to do what?" I asked, still listening to Timothy's whining in one ear.

Percy hesitated. "You must run down the Dorter and knock once on Oswald's door before Prior Oswald reaches the top of the stairs. That will bring me out, and then... well, then we'll have some explaining to do about why we are in the Dorter. Don't worry... I'll have a good story."

"You m-m-mean, you'll have a b-b-big lie to tell," I corrected, still unsure I wanted to be part of Percy's scheming.

"Steady on, Brother Gabriel," Elizabeth intervened. "Stiffen your spine, and join the plot, in a good cause, eh?"

I was shocked that Elizabeth showed precisely the same sort of bad character as Percy — maybe even worse. Both sinners and schemers. But, I wanted to trust Percy to have a good purpose in wanting to see the book. I bit my lower lip and then nodded. "Very well," I said tepidly. I heard Timothy say, "Oh my!"

Percy smiled broadly. "Good. When Ulrich arrives and we see Father Abbot and Oswald glom onto him, we'll go into action."

At mid-afternoon a man on horseback, wearing a beautifully braided uniform and red kepi hat, arrived in the forecourt, accompanied by several policemen. Captain Ulrich was much younger than I had expected, with a long thin face, square jaw, large bright eyes, and a thin, neatly-trimmed mustache. He looked stunning in his uniform. He walked like a man of confidence and authority. He also seemed rigid.

Elizabeth said she thought Ulrich looked "dreamy," but he did not appear the least tired or fatigued to me. He was perfectly alert and eager to inspect the abbey.

Just as Percy expected, Father Abbot and Prior Oswald met Captain Ulrich at the gate and guided him through the monastery, as his constant companions. All the brothers and pilgrims watched their deliberations and their tour about the abbey, including their visit to the Precipice.

When Percy confirmed that his expectations were accurate, we sprang into action. While all eyes remained on Captain Ulrich, Percy ran up the nightstairs, with me on his heels. Elizabeth took up her watch in the Cloister.

Percy dashed down the Dorter toward Prior Oswald's door, trusting that no one would be there to see him. Once at the door, he made quick work of the lock, while I took up my watch at the nightstairs. If anyone asked, I planned to say I was fetching my prayer book for afternoon hours. I could not see what Percy was doing inside the cell, of course, but later he gave me a full account.

The roughly furnished room included a bed with a straw mattress, and under the mattress, just as he had suspected, Percy found the book. I had not wanted to believe Percy's claim that Oswald lacked imagination, but hiding something under a mattress convinced me that the Prior must be one of the dimmest adults in Switzerland. Maybe in Europe.

Percy moved to the small window in Prior Oswald's wall and began to study the book, paging through and reading as he could. He saw all that Brother Paul had told and agreed with his assessment of the quality of the Latin. He saw also some of the strange words and drawings in the book — mostly plants of various kinds and some reptiles and insects — and took from his pouch a pencil and paper and began to copy some of the unusual words and symbols.

Caught between wanting to know as much as possible about the book and needing to read quickly, Percy concentrated as he had never done before. Minutes passed too quickly as he read, but he pressed on, knowing the danger of lingering.

After about an hour, the worst happened. Elizabeth sent a screeching whistle up the nightstairs. Timothy screamed. My blood froze, and then all the hairs on the back of my neck stood up and began to quiver. I ran to Oswald's door and banged once, then dashed back to a place just beside my own cell. In less than a minute, Prior Oswald appeared at the top of the nightstairs, and he immediately spied me standing in the corridor. My heart sank. Percy had not yet come out but might do so at any moment, in plain sight of Prior Oswald.

The Prior approached quickly and, even before he reached me, he demanded, "What are you doing here, Brother?" He sounded angry.

"I... er..." I said, and froze, and then said again "I-I-I... er...." All I could think was that Percy was still in Prior Oswald's room, and I had to distract the Prior from going there.

"Will you stop stuttering and answer my question, Brother Gabriel?" he insisted. "What are you doing here this time of day?"

It was then that Satan himself put it into my ear exactly what to say. A true message passed from the Prince of Darkness to me.

"I've c-c-come to find you, B-B-Brother Prior," I said, not knowing why I had come to find him.

"Why? What is it?" he asked intently, clearly thinking something was the matter.

Now that my genius for lying was in full bloom, the story came so naturally, I quite surprised myself.

"It's in the chapel, Brother Prior. I must s-s-show you something I've found there. Quick, if you please. C-C-Come with me."

I scurried past him, talking as I went. "It's something so marvelous that I must show you. Come please!" I begged, motioning him to come as I rushed toward the nightstairs.

A little way through the Dorter, I turned and was pleased to see Prior Oswald following. I was leading him away from Percy. As we reached the nightstairs, I heard him asking after me, "What is it? What's in the chapel?" He sounded even angrier.

I did not answer but descended the nightstairs as quickly as I could and then turned into the chapel. Prior Oswald came through the door behind me. I motioned. "This way, Brother Prior. This w-w-way, if you please."

I moved swiftly up the chancel toward the low altar at its end, not knowing in the slightest what I was going to say when we'd arrived at the end. There, in the light of a stained glass window, stood a large statue of Saint Hilda, or rather what she was supposed to look like. I stopped before the statue, with no place to go and unable to think what I would say when Prior Oswald finally caught up with me. In less than a minute, he huffed and sniffed and stopped behind me and said in a slow, angry voice, "Why have you brought me here, Brother Gabriel? What's the meaning of this?"

I turned to face him, and it was then that further proof of my newfound talent for telling outright falsehoods tumbled out of my mouth, even before my brain could catch up with my lying tongue.

"It's the statue, Brother Prior. The S-S-Saint," I said pointing

"What about it?" he asked, dryly, looking up at dear Hilda, who was now to witness my lying.

"I was here earlier. Praying before the Saint and asking her to pray for our Abbey and its present troubles, you see."

"Yes. Yes."

"And... er...."

"Will you stop stuttering and say what you have to say?" he demanded, impatiently.

"...and I looked up at the Saint... and... well, I s-s-s-saw...." I hesitated to know what I had seen and would tell as my final lie. "I saw her!" I exclaimed. "Yes, I saw a t-t-tear come down her cheek... a tear from her left eye." I continued pointing, my voice overcome with astonishment.

Brother Prior's mouth fell open. He goggled at the statue. Then at me. Then at the statue.

Of course, Prior Oswald thought my astonishment to be just the reaction one would have at such an apparition, but it was truly astonishment that I had thought of such a grand and stupid lie — one that would surely brand me forever as a criminal nitwit.

The Prior moved forward to look closely at the statue, his mouth still agape. He moved closer still, putting his face not six inches from the Saint's cheek.

"I see no tears," he finally said, turning toward me and peering down with a menacing scowl. "None at all. You've brought me here, at a time when I am preoccupied with important affairs of the monastery, for this?" he said, through clenched teeth. As I looked down, I saw his fingers curling into an angry fist.

I began to wilt under the heat of Prior Oswald's damning glare.

"Er... I thought i-i-it was important, Brother Prior. She was c-c-crying... and... all I could think was to fetch you to s-s-see it."

Oswald huffed and then sneered, and not bothering to utter another angry word, turned on his heels and rushed from the chapel. As I watched him retreat down the chancel, all I could think was what a fool I had made of myself and how I would be marked down as a complete lunatic by future generations of monks. 'Brother Gabriel?' They'll ask. 'Oh yes, he's that deranged young monk who went about seeing statues crying.' But then I was lifted with hope. Maybe Percy had heard my bang at the door and had escaped.

After a minute or two — when I was sure Brother Oswald had gone — I followed him out of the chapel, and, just outside in the Cloister, I found Percy and Elizabeth, standing in a group of others watching for Captain Ulrich and the Abbot to emerge from the Brew House, where Ulrich was said to be examining Father Enrico's body.

Percy and Elizabeth took me aside. "What were you and the Prior doing in the chapel?" Percy asked as Elizabeth leaned in to hear.

"Looking at the statue of Saint Hilda," I answered, sheepishly.

"Eh?" he asked.

It was then I told the entire miserable story of my lie and how Prior Oswald had made a fist and scowled at me. Percy and Elizabeth burst into laughter, revealing that neither of them was the least bit concerned about my soul and reputation.

"Well, Brother Gabriel," said Percy, taking my forearm and still smiling. "Congratulations! That was quick thinking, and you saved my life. Thank you," he said, patting me on the back.

"Your knock at the door warned me. I put the book in its hiding place, listened at the door as you and Brother Prior receded down the nightstairs, and then followed on tiptoe. I found Elizabeth at the foot of the stairs and she told me where you'd gone. And now, you are the author of a phony miracle story that will be a legend in the abbey for hundreds of years. The brothers will regard you differently from now on."

Though Percy seemed to think that a fine thing, my guilty heart found no consolation. My reputation as an imbecile and my lies would live on in the lore of the monastery.

3

For several hours, according to Brother Felix, Captain Ulrich had strutted about the monastery as if he owned it, and after examining Father Enrico's body, he soon spoke to the monks and lay-brothers who Prior Oswald had herded into the Locutory.

What Ulrich said told me that Father Abbot had convinced him what to think. "It seems this tragedy was a terrible accident, brothers," said Ulrich. "No more than that. The body of your dear pilgrim has no wounds, other than those suffered in the fall. He was not struck on the head, I am sure of that. And so there is no other conclusion to be drawn. The poor fellow wandered out to the Precipice and tumbled over by accident. It could easily happen to one not familiar with the poor footing out there."

Father Abbot smiled faintly, almost certainly because no accusation of murder would be made, and therefore no scandal would plague the abbey. Prior Oswald smiled too, which seemed painful to him.

Captain Ulrich gave permission to bury the priest, and so Father Abbot declared that we would have a funeral mass the next day and that meanwhile a grave would be prepared in the abbey cemetery, adjacent to Saint Hilda's crypt.

Prior Oswald assigned Percy to the group of lay-brothers who were to dig the grave, while Brother Felix and I joined those whose task it was to wash and prepare the body. Within the hour we had wrapped Father Enrico in his shroud, and there he lay, in the church, awaiting his funeral mass next morning, when we would sing the Requiem.

Captain Ulrich and his policemen departed just before Vespers. As I watched them leave the forecourt, I smiled relief that all seemed to be returning to the normal tranquility of our community, or at least there was some feeling of that in the air.

As I recall it now, we were almost finished chanting Vespers, when suddenly old Brother Paul began to scream hysterically and then ran about the Chapel, bumping into the monks and seizing the arms of one or another. This strange behaviour lasted only a minute or so, before the poor old brother fell to the floor, holding his head with both hands and then passed out. The first thing that came into my mind was that Moloch — the demon Brother Felix had named — must have seized poor Brother Paul.

Brother Francis, the apothecary, who tends to our medical needs, fell to his knees to see to Brother Paul, while the rest of us began to pray, as Father Abbot instructed.

"We must take him to the infirmary," said Brother Francis, and so several of the monks took up the old man in their arms and carried him up to our small infirmary, just beyond the Dorter. Later, Brother Francis reported that Brother Paul was resting quietly and that the doctor had come from Chaumont to attend to him. They suspected, we heard, that Brother Paul has suffered apoplexy, but almost immediately the monks began to whisper that he'd been overcome by the demon Moloch, who was now moving freely about the abbey, perhaps in the guise of one of the pilgrims. Later, as I prepared for sleep, I was struck by one thought. Ever since the book had gone missing, our abbey had known no peace.

Percy and the filthy, grave-digging brothers returned, exhausted, in time to pray Compline. Percy explained they were chipping out a grave in solid rock. Hard work.

When they had finished the grave, the lay-brothers went down to the Aarn, dropped their robes, and jumped into the frigid waters to bathe. It was there, Percy told me later — in the icy jolt of the river's water — that he knew what we must do next.

"What?" I asked, almost afraid to hear it, and still thinking that a demon had seized poor Brother Paul.

"I must see Albertus — the hermit."

Chapter Ten
Wherein Father Abbot Refuses

10 April 1911

1

"That's impossible!" I protested. "In case you have not noticed it, we are cloistered monks. Well, I am anyway. You are more or less a prisoner here, because of your past sinfulness. Anyway, it means we may not come and go as we please, and it certainly means that we are not allowed to just up and go visit a hermit. And, in case you misunderstand that word, Percy, a hermit is a person who does not welcome visitors."

"We both know there's one person who visits Albertus. The lay-brother, Johann. He goes each month. Right?"

"True, but Johann merely fulfills the monastery's charitable work of supporting Albertus. Johann does not visit Albertus. He told me he just leaves his supplies where the hermit will find them and then returns."

"Exactly... and we are going to accompany him next time, only we are going to visit Albertus." Percy smiled. "While we were digging the grave, Johann told me he will soon make his journey. We will be his companions."

"No. We can go nowhere without Father Abbot's permission, and you know very well, he won't allow it. He won't," I repeated. Still, I could see that my objections meant nothing to Percy. Something about the steely look in his eyes told me he was determined.

"Very well," I continued, crossing my arms. "How do you propose to get the Abbot's permission? Knowing, as we both do, that he won't give it? Johann would never guide us without it, and only he knows how to find Albertus."

"Gabriel, sometimes you surprise me by your good thinking. You are quicker with your wit than you seem."

I didn't know whether to be angry or pleased with Percy's backhanded compliment. I decided to be direct. "You still haven't told me how you plan to gain Father Abbot's permission."

"That's because I don't yet know myself, but I'm working on that. Oh yes. I am working on that even now."

2

The next morning, Percy and I answered the bell for Terce and joined the brothers in the Cloister. Our chanting and praying proceeded in the usual, peaceful fashion, I was pleased to see. When it ended and we prepared to disperse for our assigned work, Prior Oswald took Percy aside. His face seemed even sterner than usual, which was saying something, for Prior Oswald's face always resembled a donkey with a stomach full of sour apples. Then, I noticed he showed bright red blotches all over his face and hands, which he scratched incessantly. Whatever could be the matter with him, I wondered.

"I know you're snooping around, Brother Percy," he said, in a frenzied voice. "Snooping for some reason after the book, eh."

Percy was taken aback. He realized Prior Oswald was about to deliver one of his severe warnings.

"Yes, it's true I have asked some questions about it. After all, I was suspected of taking it, and it interests me... to know more about it."

Prior Oswald drew himself up to his full height and narrowed his eyes, the crimson blotches on his face even redder. "That book is none of your concern, Brother Percy. It's enough that it has been found, and of course, you are no longer suspected. Father Enrico took it, though I cannot imagine how or why. Still, there it is."

"That's exactly what I have wondered, Brother Prior. How came it to be in Father Enrico's rucksack?"

Oswald's eyes flashed. "Enough! You need not pursue such questions. It's upsetting to the community to do so. To the pilgrims — our guests. You will stop your inquiries. Do you understand?"

"Yes, sir. I understand," said Percy, looking at his feet.

Prior Oswald said no more. He turned on his heel and disappeared into the Refectory, scratching his blotches as he went.

I had been watching the two from across the Cloister, and it was only later Percy told me what the Prior had said. Still, I could tell the Prior was angry, just looking at his face. So could Sister Rose, who was also watching. When Percy joined me to go to our chores, she hailed us.

"I could not help seeing the Prior scolding you, Brother Percy. About your interest in the stolen book?" she inquired. Sister Rose's suggestion surprised Percy at first. "Don't be surprised. The pilgrims say you've been asking questions."

"Yes. He's angry with me. Says it's upsetting the abbey."

"Aye lad, but why the interest in that old book? After all, the abbey has recovered it, and all's well, eh? No more bother, surely. Besides, I can tell ye, the Saint herself has spoken into my mind, and she says she is pleased."

Percy smiled. "Yes, I suppose so. Best left well enough alone. As you say, all's well."

The old nun smiled and continued on her way with Sister Fiona.

"What was that about?" I thought, looking after the jolly Irish nuns as they continued toward the Guest House.

"Percy," I asked, "did you see those horrible red blotches on Prior Oswald's face? And his scratching?"

Percy smiled, but before he could answer, Elizabeth walked up. "Prior Oswald's in a bad way. Must be suffering a dread disease. Everyone's talking about it. Looks terrible, poor man. Scratching all the time."

"Yes," I said. "I was just asking Percy," who was still smiling.

"I haven't the slightest idea," he answered. "Must be painful, whatever it is."

Just then, Elizabeth's face darkened, with a strange expression I'd not seen before. Percy noticed it too. "What is it?" he asked.

"What's what?"

"That odd look on your face."

"Oh, that." She paused, as if hesitating to explain. "I'm starting to worry about some of the people around here."

"How do you mean?"

"They're seeing things. Demons and other apparitions. Ever since the book went missing. Hearing voices too. Creeping insanity maybe? This place is getting spookier all the time, and I think some of the people around here are going to be carted off to the asylum."

I looked down at my feet. Percy said nothing. She continued.

"I don't doubt that soon some of the inmates here will start reporting angels fluttering about the place."

I sensed it was time to leave. "Well, I must be off," I explained. "It's my time to help in the Refectory."

Percy and Elizabeth lingered and watched me depart. I learned later what was said between them.

"Listen, Elizabeth. Promise to keep a secret? About what I'm about to tell you? It's sensitive information."

Elizabeth stiffened and her eyes narrowed. "Secrets, eh? Very well. I'll take my oath. They may torture me for days, and I will not tell," she said solemnly, holding up her right hand.

"No need for that. Just keep your mouth shut about it, and do as I say, and that'll be good enough."

"What is it?"

"Those blotches on Prior Oswald?"

"Yes. What?"

Percy took a small vial from his marsupium — a pouch monks wear around their waists.

"Yesterday, before I left the Prior's room, I poured a powder from this vial on his blanket and mattress."

"A powder?"

"Pulverized nettle — mixed with other ingredients of my own invention. Sleeping on it last night is the source of poor Prior Oswald's sad affliction."

Elizabeth gasped. Then, eyes bulging, she put both hands to her mouth. "Oh my! Those are hives... from the nettle. I've had that myself, just from touching the leaves."

"Oh, my little concoction will render a far worse condition. Poor man has probably breathed in a good dose of the powder and probably rubbed it in his eyes too," Percy explained, with no hint of remorse.

Elizabeth looked at him from the corner of her eye. "Brother Percy, you are some relation to Satan himself. What are you doing in a monastery? I'm starting to believe all the nonsense about a demon in this monastery, and I suspect the demon is you. Otherwise, why would you do such a thing to Prior Oswald?"

Percy looked hurt. "I'm not evil. There's great good to be achieved from the Prior's affliction."

"What?" she asked, doubtfully.

"For one thing, I want to give Oswald something to think about, other than me. I particularly don't want him interfering in something I am going to ask of Father Abbot. But now, I also learn that Gabriel is guilty-minded about what he told the Prior yesterday. You know — that story about the crying Saint."

"What of it?"

"That's where you come in. You know how gossip-crazy this place is. Tell one monk and all will know it in about ten minutes. And they'll believe anything, as long as it's somehow mystical."

"Yes."

"I want you to help me seed a rumor among the pilgrims and monks — a rumor that will help Brother Gabriel."

"Sure. What rumor?" she asked, quietly excited.

"We're going to suggest that Prior Oswald has been afflicted by the Saint herself — yes, Saint Hilda — because he ridiculed Gabriel's account of her tears. Saint Hilda is offended, you see, that her tears were scoffed at."

Elizabeth's face darkened. "Percy, you are a demon... but I think your desire to help poor Gabriel is commendable. Very sweet too. I'll gladly help."

"Good. You are responsible to tell the story around the Guest House and be sure to tell Brother Jean-Baptiste. He's the abbey's champion gossip."

They smiled and shook hands, then parted to spread their tale. Within the hour, Percy and I were once more working together at chores, when Brother Felix approached, his face full of news.

"Do you know what's being said?" he asked in a confidential undertone, his eyes darting from side to side.

"What?" Percy asked.

"Prior Oswald has been struck down by the Saint herself because he disbelieved her tears. That's what. Imagine," he said, a worried look on his face.

When Brother Felix continued on his way, I looked at Percy in dismay. "But it cannot be. I made up the story of the tears. It was a big lie and almost certainly sinful."

"Brother Gabriel," Percy explained, "saints work in strange ways that we mortals cannot know. I believe Saint Hilda herself was using you to express her anxiety about what's happening here. That's what I think," he said, shaking his head.

Not long after that, we heard that Brother Jerome, an aged Italian monk, had gone to the chapel to observe the Saint's statue, and soon returned to the Warming Room in a fluster, testifying that he too had seen the tears. Some of the brothers rushed to the chapel to confirm the apparition, and at least one said afterward that he too had seen a tear on the Saint's cheek.

Later that day, Father Abbot hurried to the chapel and looked for a long while at the statue. Though he confessed he could not see tears, he nonetheless decided to declare a vigil of prayer in the Saint's chapel, to begin immediately.

I was entirely confused by these goings-on, but soon I concluded that although I had made up the story, it was probably an inspiration from the Saint. And to think she had struck down Prior Oswald with those terrible blisters because he scoffed.

As I was considering how the Saint had used me to convey her message, Brother Francis emerged from the nightstairs. "Oh, Brother Percy," he hailed from behind us. "Brother Percy."

We turned as he approached. "Ah, just the person I hoped to see. Father Abbot has asked me to find you."

"Oh?" said Percy.

"Oh, yes. He wishes to see you. In his rooms."

"How is Brother Paul?" Percy asked. I was wondering the same thing.

"Not well, I think. He is old, and the excitement of whatever caused his distress continues to afflict him. Doctor Friedmann orders complete rest, and so that's what we are giving. We shall see," he said and then sighed.

When Brother Francis had walked on, Percy turned to me. "What do you suppose the Abbot wants?"

"I don't know, but I'd guess he wants to lecture you on your monastic discipline. In case you have not noticed, you are far from an ideal monk. I hesitate to tell you, Percy, but you seem to lack spiritual purpose."

Percy looked at me. "Did Timothy tell you that? He's been criticizing me behind my back, again, hasn't he?"

I was taken aback by the question, I admit. "Ah... Timothy says you are a shame to your own guardian angel who mostly spends his time avoiding eye contact with his fellow guardian angels."

"Where is Timothy now?"

I looked around. "Over there by the hedge."

Percy turned toward the hedge and gave it a look. I would say Percy's look smacked of willful defiance, and it told me that he and Timothy were having a tense relationship.

"Does Timothy know why Father Abbot wants to see me?" he asked.

"No. He never knows things like that, or at least, if he does, he keeps a closed mouth."

"Lot of good he is to me right now, then," Percy said, looking once more toward the hedge.

"That boy is a walking collection of bad attitudes," I heard Timothy say into my mind. "Little wonder his own guardian angel is an emotional mess."

"I suppose I had best get myself up to Father Abbot's rooms," Percy continued. "He'll be even angrier if I'm slow to respond to his summons."

He walked toward the nightstairs. I said after him, "Good luck, Percy. I will pray for you."

Percy turned and smiled.

"Better to pray for Father Abbot," Timothy quipped. "No telling what Percy will talk the poor fellow into doing."

3

As Percy approached the Abbot's door, he at first hesitated to knock. Plucking up his courage, he rapped once, and from inside there came an instant, "Yes. Come in."

The rough oak door creaked on its ancient hinges, and the sound reminded Percy of his last dreadful visit to the Abbot's cell. The room, furnished only with a simple table, two rough-made chairs, and bookcase, was a study of sorts, for it was stacked high with old books, many of them on the table. In one corner stood a small fireplace, with a crackling fire in the grate, and in the wall beside it, a small window. Through an open door to the other room, Percy could see a simple cot, with a straw mattress. Father Abbot, his long face as grim as ever, sat at the table, and as soon as Percy entered, he said, "Take that chair, Brother Percy. Please."

"Yes. Thank you, sir," said Percy, dreading to hear why he'd been summoned. He did not have long to wait.

"I'm told you are making further inquiries about the book that went missing, Brother. Why is that? Why do you continue to trouble yourself about it? And trouble the monastery about it. After all, the book has been found and... well... any suspicions... any suspicions some might have had about you are now proved wrong. So, that's an end to it, don't you see."

"No. I am not sure that is an end to it, Father Abbot."

"What?" he asked, dismayed and annoyed.

"No, not an end at all," said Percy. "In fact, if my suspicions are correct, there'll be yet another attempt on the book and perhaps followed by an even greater tragedy." As Percy watched the Abbot's face, he considered how much of his suspicions he should tell. Percy is a master at reading faces, mostly in the interest of his sinful ways of duping people.

"I don't understand what you mean," the Abbot continued.

"I mean this, Father Abbot. I disagree with Captain Ulrich's quick conclusion that Father Enrico died by mischance. Accident? No, not at all. He was pushed."

Father Abbot stood, his eyes flashing his consternation. "That's preposterous! You have no call to suggest that." He glared.

"I do indeed," Percy protested, "if you will pardon me for disagreeing."

"Well then, what is your justification? Your evidence?" the Abbot challenged, folding his arms and raising his chin defiantly. It was a good thing for Percy that Abbot Bartholomew is a German who loves debate. Brother Percy had been hoping to make his case, and he pounced with glee, now that Father Abbot invited him to do so.

"Two things, Father Abbot. The first is the nonsense that Father Enrico should wander out to the Precipice and then somehow fall over, based entirely on the evidence that he had no injuries other than those from a fall. If he had gone out there to meet someone, that person could easily have surprised him and pushed him over. Father Enrico was a small man. Even I could have overpowered him. So, there's the question of what he was doing at the Precipice."

Father Abbot unfolded his arms and continued to listen in silence.

"And then there's the rucksack and the notion Father Enrico was about to run away with the book."

"Yes. That seems to make sense to me, as it did to Captain Ulrich," said the Abbot, tersely.

"Another easy and unwarranted conclusion. If Father Enrico was prepared to flee, why did he take with him none of his belongings? Brother Gabriel and I looked in his room in the Guest House. He left behind almost all of his things, including a gold watch that was clearly a family item."

Father Abbot's face suddenly lost its icy stare. "Then what? What are you saying, Brother Percy? There's a murderer among us?"

"I am suggesting that Father Enrico, for some reason, was lured to the Precipice to meet someone — possibly an accomplice in the theft of the book — and he was pushed over. And that somehow the rucksack with the book went with him. Those are assumptions that fit the available evidence. But why was he killed? Who killed him? And, if the intention all along was to steal the book, why was it allowed to go over the Precipice? Those are all things I do not yet understand... questions that demand answers," Percy said, frowning and leaning forward.

Percy's logic stunned the Abbot, whose mouth now fell agog with dismay. He said nothing for the longest while, as he turned and gazed out his small window, staring blankly into the distance. When he finally spoke, he could only utter, "*Mein Gott im Himmel!*" He whispered it mainly to himself.

"If what I suspect is true," Percy continued, "there is a murderer in this abbey right now, and who knows what that person is planning? If the one who murdered Father Enrico somehow failed to secure the book, he may be waiting to try again, and perhaps he'll murder again."

Except for the occasional flight into speculations of various kinds, there is nothing as appealing to a German as cold logic, and that is precisely what Percy had just served up to Abbot Bartholomew. It stunned him like a poleax between the eyes, and especially the part about another murder. When he eventually recovered, he could only ask, "But, what now? Shall I summon Captain Ulrich again? Ask him to reconsider?"

"What now, Father Abbot, is to find out what's going on here, and I believe that — whatever it is — that the book is at the center of it. That's why I am questioning, no matter that the book has been recovered."

"Well, Brother Percy, I can assure you that Prior Oswald had taken infinite precautions to hide that book where none shall find it. There's no danger of theft, eh? None," he repeated, emphatically.

It was here that Percy stopped telling all he knew or suspected, except for one thing.

"Father Abbot," he said, with a plea in his voice. Percy is expert at getting just the right tone of innocent pleading in his voice. I might add that Percy never pleaded, except as a cheap trick to lull an unsuspecting victim into something. "Father Abbot," he repeated, a pitiful look on his face. "I have prayed over this problem, harder than I have ever prayed, and I believe I have been moved to do one thing more to investigate poor Father Enrico's death."

"Yes," said the Abbot. "And that is?"

"I must see Albertus."

The Abbot, who had returned to his chair, sprang to his feet again. "You what! That's impossible. Albertus is a hermit, and we have taken it as a spiritual work of our monastery to support him in his holiness." Then, looking sternly at Percy and squarely into his eyes, he added, grimly, "In case you do not fathom it, Brother Percy, it may even be sinful to disturb a hermit. Why on earth would you wish to disturb him?"

"I believe from what I've been told by Brother Paul that Albertus knows more about that book than any person alive — things that may explain why Father Enrico was killed, even who killed him, and why that person was unable to take the book with him."

Father Abbot sat down hard in his chair. He had no arguments left to use with Percy. He seemed exhausted and remained silent and looking blankly at the hearth fire for some minutes. Percy continued.

"Brother Johann travels each month to Albertus' hermitage in the high mountains, to deliver supplies and to collect firewood. He leaves in two days. Please, Father Abbot. Allow Brother Gabriel and me to accompany him and to learn what the hermit is able to tell. I promise you, I will only speak to Albertus if he agrees to be disturbed. It may prevent a further tragedy," he added. "Possibly even another murder."

Abbot Bartholomew remained silent, clearly thinking about all Percy had said and considering the strange request he'd made. His face remained grave, his eyes sad. Finally, he spoke with conviction.

"Brother Percy, what you say has some merit, but I believe we now know all we need to know about the missing book. Father Enrico took it, probably for money, and died by accident before he could make good his escape. Now, thanks to God, we have our book, and Prior Oswald will safeguard it better. And that is an end to it."

Then, standing, he continued, "Brother Percy, you may not visit Albertus! There is no need, except your own curiosity, to disturb him. No. You may not go."

Percy had reached the end of his schemes, and he knew it. Well, almost the end. In fact, he had only one ploy remaining — a desperate idea. Facing Abbot Bartholomew, he asked, "Am I not a lay-brother of this community, Father Abbot?"

"Why, yes, Brother Percy, you certainly are. But what does that have to do with Albertus?"

"In that case," said Percy, "I appeal to Trial by Cross*."

Chapter Eleven

Wherein Percy Endures
the Trial by Cross

1

"You what!"

Percy had just demanded something very unusual, and Father Abbot could not believe it.

"Brother Percy, consider what you are saying. What you demand is something that has not been done in 900 years. You cannot mean what you say."

Percy said nothing. After several minutes of tense silence, Father Abbot declared, "Very well, Brother. Tomorrow, after Lauds, you will have your Trial by Cross, and God Himself will decide your case."

2

Word of Percy's dramatic action spread quickly through the abbey. Many of the brothers, including me, had no notion at first of what Percy had done, but soon we learned — from more knowledgeable brothers — just what had happened.

Percy, it was said, had invoked a provision of the Monastery's Charter, which came down from Charlemagne himself, in 792. It ordered that in disputes between ecclesiastics — between monks or between monasteries — either party could appeal to Trial by Cross. In his disagreement with Abbot Bartholomew, Percy had claimed this right.

"But what is Trial by Cross?" I asked Brother Jerome, as several of the brothers gathered around to learn.

'It's an ordeal," he explained, "in which the two parties stand on either side of the cross. Both outstretch their arms, and there they must stand until one drops his arms. The one who remains with his arms outstretched, it is assumed, prevailed because God Himself willed it."

"Do you mean that Father Abbot must...?"

"No. Either party may appoint a champion, and because Father Abbot is clearly too old for such an ordeal, he will certainly do so. Percy could do likewise if he wished."

"Good Heavens!" I could only say. "What will come of that?"

<h1 style="text-align:center">3</h1>

The next morning, after Lauds, while all the brothers were gathered in the chapel, Father Abbot called Percy forward.

"Brother Percy," he explained, "has appealed to Trial by Cross, to settle a disagreement between us, as is his right according to our ancient Charter. In this ordeal, Brother Anthony will take my part."

Brother Anthony, a young Italian monk who was known for his strength, came forward and stood opposite Percy. Father Abbot looked at both.

"Brothers, extend your arms," he ordered, and both did as they were told. "Now," the Abbot said, "God will decide."

Father Abbot ordered that one monk should remain in the chapel at all times during the ordeal to witness the outcome of the trial.

Many of the monks lingered to observe the strange trial. Most seemed to believe that the competition would surely end within the hour, but the hour came and both brothers continued to stand, arms outstretched. As the monks began to disperse to breakfast, I decided to remain. When the others returned at Prime (7:00 a.m.), they found the two continuing to stand.

It seemed strange to me that, as we chanted our prayers, the two brothers stood in the long chancel of our chapel, with arms outstretched — a pained expression on both faces. A few of the monks remained after prayers, but most like me had to go to their assigned chores.

As we observed all the Hours throughout that day, the brothers continued to stand. At Compline (6 p.m.), there was a great difference. Brother Anthony's face appeared contorted — anguished — and his eyes full of pain. Percy's face, however, appeared placid; his eyes fixed in a vacant stare. At first, I was confused by Percy, but then I knew that somehow he had gone into a trance, by which he had escaped from his pain — into some place that gave him peace. They had been standing twelve hours.

As we prayed, Brother Anthony responded to the chanting by starting to groan, almost in harmony with our chant. It was both eerie and disturbing to hear it, especially as his suffering grew louder. Not ten minutes into our prayers, he commenced to sway side-to-side, and then to scream. Finally, his arms dropped and the poor brother collapsed in a heap on the cold stone floor. There he lay, half-conscious and still groaning.

Several of the brothers rushed to his aid, one with a skin of brandy to revive him. Father Abbot ordered him taken to the Infirmary for care.

Then, he turned to Percy, who continued to stand, oblivious to all that had just happened. "Brother Percy!" he shouted. Percy jolted from his trance, looked about to see that Brother Anthony had gone, and then collapsed also onto the floor. One of the brothers rushed forward, once more with brandy, and without being ordered, some lifted Brother Percy to his feet and off to the Infirmary with Brother Anthony.

When Percy had gone, Father Abbot waited until the chapel had returned to silence. Then, stone-faced and clearly disappointed, he said, "God's will is done. Brother Percy has prevailed."

The next day, Father Abbot summoned Percy to his study. "God has decided in your favor, Brother Percy. You may go to Albertus, as you wish. If you are right about Father Enrico — that he was murdered — it may avert another tragedy. Go then, and give this letter to Albertus," he said, handing Percy a note. "It asks him to answer your questions. But you must do as I instruct. Leave this note with his supplies. Albertus will find it, and if he is willing to speak to you, he will decide. Wait for him to respond, and under no circumstances are you to intrude upon his solitude. Is that clear, Brother Percy? It must be his decision."

"Yes, Father Abbot," he said. "I agree."

"Good. Now go. And — "

"Yes."

"Take care, Brother Percy. Just... take care," he said and then turned to look into the hearth fire.

Chapter Twelve
Wherein We Find the Talking Tree

11 April 1911

1

Word of our pending departure spread quickly in the gossip mill of the abbey, though none but Percy and I knew precisely why we would accompany Brother Johann. Speculation abounded, and some of it said we were going to deliver a letter from Father Abbot, asking Albertus to pray for the abbey, and especially for Prior Oswald, whose condition had worsened and had confined him to his cot.

No one made much of it, but I was inwardly excited to be making my first adventure beyond the abbey's gates since I'd come to St. Ambrose ten years earlier. My first real look at the world beyond.

As Percy and I packed our rucksacks for the journey, Johann came into the Dorter, an odd look on his face.

"One of the pilgrims wishes to see you, Percy. In the Warming Room."

"Pilgrim?" Percy questioned.

"Aye. The French girl."

Percy finished quickly and, swinging his pack over his shoulder, said, "I'll meet you two in the Cloister."

When he reached the foot of the nightstairs, he found Elizabeth waiting, just outside the Warming Room.

"So you're going? No stopping you, eh?" she said, a worried look in her eyes.

"Yes. There's no other way. We must learn what Albertus knows about the book, and the only way is to talk to him. No other way," Percy repeated.

"In that case, I wish you good fortune and God's speed, Percy." She took his hand.

"I wish you could go with us."

"No. I would only slow you down and maybe even get you killed," she lamented, looking down at her foot. "I'm not made for climbing mountains, but that doesn't mean I couldn't if I had to do it," she insisted, frowning.

"Oh, I am certain of that," Percy agreed, with conviction and a smile. "I know you can do anything you set your mind to, Elizabeth." She squeezed his hand.

"Besides, Papa would never hear of it. And Mama would faint."

"I see," Percy said, not knowing what else was to be said.

Suddenly Elizabeth threw her arms around Percy's neck and kissed his cheek, and then scurried toward the Guest House on her crutch. Half-way down the path, she turned, looked back, and smiled faintly, and then waved.

Percy smiled back and waved his good-bye.

It was a long moment before Percy heard someone behind him cough. Wheeling around, he saw me and Johann.

"It's time, Percy," said Johann. "The morning's getting on and we must make more than halfway before dark."

In the forecourt, we found waiting for us a donkey — straining unhappily under the burden of our supplies for the hermit. Johann smiled broadly to see him and said, "Brothers, may I present Jonah? He has been my companion so many times to resupply the hermit that I believe he could find his way on his own."

"Pardon me for saying so," said Percy, "but Jonah appears so old and frail, I fear he'll not make this trek, even with our help."

I did not like to say so, but Percy was right. Jonah was the prefect specimen of a donkey who'd seen better days. Small, skinny, ears drooping — Jonah did not seem the least bit enthusiastic about our mission to find Albertus.

"Never you mind Jonah's looks, Brothers. He's the finest, most sure-footed alpine donkey I've ever known. He'll make the trek — no fear," Johann smiled, as he took Jonah's lead and moved forward.

As we crossed the stone bridge beyond the gates, I looked back once more to see its portal, with those reassuring words of Saint Ambrose upon it. Awash in the excitement of venturing beyond the abbey for the first time in my memory, I uttered a prayer and then looked about to see Timothy walking behind us. We first walked east along the main road that leads to Lichtenstein and Austria. After several kilometers, Johann turned north, onto a rougher trek that would take us into the Forest of Ohme and then beyond, across the broad valley of the Aarn and up — always up — into the high mountains.

2

Our path, a narrow wagon rut, led us deep into the dreaded forest. I began to recall all the stories I'd heard about the place — its demons and their many evil deeds. The forest grew denser as we walked, and soon its canopy was so thick it blocked much of the light. Though I knew it was morning, it began to seem like evening. As we walked, the atmosphere of the forest grew damper, and a thick, musty odor of fungus and decay filled our nostrils.

Less than a kilometer into the darkness, the strange noises began. Johann, in the lead, perked-up and looked to the thick undergrowth on either side of our path. Jonah's ears perk up also.

"W-W-What is it?" I asked.

Johann stopped, and when he turned I didn't like the worried look I saw on his face. "The demons, Brother. I always hear them as I get into the thick of the forest. Demons for sure. Be on your guard."

"Will the demons attack us?" I asked, looking side-to-side.

No answer.

The noises, which sometimes sounded almost like human cries, continued the whole while we made our way through the forest. It seems odd to say it about a donkey, but Jonah had a worried look in his eyes. "Maybe we should pray as we go?" I suggested and so we chanted our hymns, to drown out the moans and cries of the demons. Or were they the cries of the lost souls that demons had captured?

Soon, we came upon a narrow brook, trickling across our path. Though it seemed shallow and harmless, Johann stopped and gazed cautiously at it.

"What is it?" I asked. He said nothing.

"Easy, Brother," I heard Timothy say.

Then, I heard it. A low gurgling sound at first, but then louder and louder. The sound of bubbling. We stood wondering what it could be, and then we saw. The quiet little brook erupted into a boil, like a cauldron of water on a hot fire. The boiling grew, as steam rose from the water, and the dampness of the forest wrapped us in a thick, warm fog, which seemed to glow.

We backed away from the boiling stream, and, as the sound of the bubbling became a deafening din, we fell to our knees and covered our ears with our hands. Jonah also backed away, his ears standing straight up and his tail too.

I looked up and there stood Percy, silhouetted against the glow, his staff in one hand, but in his other, holding up to the boiling fog, a rough cross he'd taken from inside his tunic.

The brook boiled violently for only a minute or so, and then as quickly as they had come, the turbulence and noise faded. In the eerie quiet that followed, the mist lifted and the little brook resumed its gentle flow and delicate babble.

"Gabriel," Percy said, still looking at the water, while Johann and I remained trembling on our knees. Well, I was trembling anyway.

"Yes."

"Remind me to apologize to Brother Felix. There might just be something to that Forest of Demons business he tells."

After a few moments, Johann spoke. "Let's go. No time to waste," he urged, coming to his feet and stepping into the water, tugging on the lead of a reluctant Jonah. I feared the water would rise again and boil us alive, so I followed cautiously.

3

In only two hours' time, we reached the other side of the Demon Forest and the darkness began to lift. At a wide place in our path, we came to a giant oak tree, standing strangely, I thought, in the very middle of the path, where it must have been for hundreds of years. As we approached it, a voice pleaded, "Help me!"

At first, we did not know where the voice had come from. We looked to both sides of the path and then leaned to peer around the tree. Then, up in the tree. Nothing. But, then it became clear. The frightened voice came from inside the tree!

"Help me!" the voice repeated. "Help me!"

Then it came to me. It was the voice of a child — a girl.

Percy stepped forward. "Who are you? How may we help you?" he asked, still looking around as he spoke.

"Elsie," came the quick reply. "I'm Elsie."

"Easy, Brother," I heard Johann whisper. "The demons are full of tricks."

"Why does your voice come from the tree?" asked Percy, his eyes still darting about.

"I came into the forest to play," she whined, "and the demon tricked me. He locked me in the tree. Help me," she pleaded.

"How?" Percy asked. "How can we help you?"

She began to cry. Clearly confused, Percy looked around at me and then at Johann. Then his eyes flashed excitement. "Gabriel, this is one for Timothy. Ask him what we must do."

I turned and spied Timothy standing several meters behind us, a confused look on his face.

"Now, let me get this straight. Percy St.-John wishes to know what I think he should do. Is that right? Am I hearing this question correctly? he asked into my mind.

"Yes. That's the idea," I said, knowing that Timothy was suspecting a cheap trick.

There was a pause, and then Timothy said, "Do what monks do."

When I told Percy what Timothy had said, Percy frowned. "I'm getting just a tad disappointed with that guardian angel of yours, Gabriel. He...." Percy stopped himself in mid-sentence.

"He what, Percy?" I asked. "What is it?"

Just then the voice from the tree pleaded, "Help me!"

"You tell me, Gabriel. Johann? What do monks do?"

I had to think, and then it came to me.

"Monks pray, Percy."

"Exactly!" he said.

On Percy's instructions, we circled the tree, each standing on one side and linking our hands around it. We closed our eyes and began to chant the prayers of Nones, which was about what time it was. I heard distant thunder as we began to chant, and then saw a flash of lightning over the forest, followed by a gust of wind that almost blew us off our feet. When we had finished, we opened our eyes and each fell back. The tree had vanished and in its place, stood a young girl — not ten years old. I don't know why, but she ran immediately to me and latched on for dear life.

I could not pry her loose, nor did I want to, so comforted was she to hang onto me. She sobbed mindlessly for the longest while, as we three brothers gazed at each other in disbelief. Finally, it was Percy who spoke.

"Elsie, you are among friends now. We are brothers of the monastery."

The girl's sobbing slowly subsided, and yet she continued to cling to me.

"Elsie, where is your home?" Percy asked. "How long have you been here? In the forest?"

At first, she did not answer, but then she sobbed, "Two years, I think."

I am sure my own mouth fell open, along with Johann's. Even Percy's eyes grew wide.

"I live in the valley," she said, "not far from the forest. My family is there," she explained, pointing up the path.

I could see by the look on his face that Brother Johann remained suspicious of the girl. That she was a demon. But Percy cared more about getting beyond the forest.

"Let's go, brothers," he warned. "The demons will want their revenge on us for releasing the girl."

We hoisted our rucksacks. Elsie took my hand, and we continued down the path and toward the light.

In time, we emerged into the broad valley formed by the River Aarn. Not one-half hour into the valley we came to the gate of a well-kept little cottage. When Elsie saw it she began to scream with joy. Our shouts brought a woman through the cottage door, and when she spied Elsie, she screamed and ran toward us, screeching. Hearing the ruckus, a man — her husband I guessed — came out of the cottage and seeing the cause of the commotion, he too ran toward us.

The two swept Elsie up in their arms and smothered her in kisses and hugs, with such wailing and praising God they did not even notice our presence. When finally the woman — still sobbing and wailing, "My baby!" — saw us, she fell upon me, her arms about my neck, lavishing kisses on my cheeks and forehead.

Johann did not like to linger more than necessary, but Percy took time to explain to the girl's parents how we'd found Elsie in the forest and how we'd rescued her from the demons. As we finally continued on our way up the wagon trace, I looked back to see the three, still hugging and laughing and rejoicing.

The narrow road took us past farms and crofts. Later, as we began our climb, I looked back across the valley, and in the great distance, I could see the abbey, perched upon its prominence, its red tile roofs vivid in the crisp mountain air and shimmering in the late-morning sun. It must have been a grim foreboding, but at that moment I thought I might be seeing our beloved abbey for the last time. So far, I sighed, the outside world that I had longed to see was a frightening place.

Chapter Thirteen

Wherein I Flee

From the Tatzelwurm Monster

1

In little more than an hour of rapid walking, we reached rougher terrain. Brother Johann, the mountaineer, set a hard pace as we began to climb — now, always climbing — relentlessly to the north and not knowing when or how far he would take us. Ahead, we could see the high mountains, their snow caps glistening in the midday sun, and everything bathed in misty hues of blue and pink.

Now, our path narrowed and began to hug the side of the mountain. Looking out to my right, I often marveled how high we'd climbed above the valley below. Sometimes the path was but a meter wide, and with my heavy rucksack, I feared that if my load shifted, it would surely take me over the side.

Even more troubling, we now began to hear the rumble of distant thunder, followed quickly by a noticeable darkening of the sky. Clouds — black clouds — rolled in from the north and soon we found ourselves in a torrent of rain, attended by loud claps of thunder and bolts of lightning. Worse still, all this came with a wind that seemed determined to blow us off the mountain.

There was no sheltering from the storm. Johann urged us on and always up the narrow path. We continued in this way, soaked to the marrow, for at least an hour, when as rapidly as it had come, the storm passed and in its place there emerged a beautiful spring day.

Then too, the path soon opened more broadly into a mountain glen, where we found trees and scrub vegetation, and where the walking was easier. By late afternoon, we came to a stream, its icy water pouring off the mountains and rushing across our path. To our left, we could see the falls, cascading off the mountain, and to our right, we could hear the stream falling with a great noise into the valley below, though vegetation and rocks concealed just how far downstream those lower falls began. The stream looked impassable, and I remembered with fright the little brook in the Forest of Ohme. Brother Johann paused and then took off his rucksack. He looked worried. Percy and I did the same, though not knowing why.

The noise of rushing water and the falls beyond made it difficult to hear Brother Johann's instructions, and the spray from the upstream falls hit my face, stinging like little icy needles.

"The stream is rapid," Johann shouted, "but it's not deep. We can ford it up to our thighs, but we must hold the rucksacks on our shoulders to keep them dry." The big monk looked back at me, as I struggled to shoulder my burden. "Take care the force of the water does not sweep you along, little Brother. The falls you're hearing below are only twenty meters downstream. Lose your footing and you'll go over for sure."

Handing one end of his rope to Percy and me, Brother Johann started into the stream, his staff in his right hand, holding high his rucksack with the other, the rope tied around his chest. Jonah followed, his pack partly submerged in the stream.

Once across, Johann shouted above the noise of falls, "Take hold of the rope, first Gabriel and then you last, Brother Percy." That done, I moved gingerly into the stream, and in no time I was waist deep in the rushing waters, feeling the stream's frigid grip and the force of its undercurrent. Percy came last. I did not look back, but I heard him screech as he felt the first icy embrace of the stream. "A mountain baptism, Brothers," Johann shouted. "And a cold one," he added. Still soaked from the recent storm, it did not seem to matter much that we would get another drenching.

Halfway across the ten meters of the stream I felt a strong undertow. Then, in the next moment, the current swept me entirely off my feet. Worse, I'd lost my hold on the rope. I felt myself sliding down the stream, bouncing off its rocky bottom, holding onto my rucksack. The sudden shock of the frigid water caused my mind to go black. I awakened to my own screaming. "Help!" I begged, as I bobbed to the surface again, briefly. It was then I felt the force of something pulling me against the push of the stream, and, as I looked back, I could see Percy, holding the strap of my rucksack with one arm and straining every muscle to pull me back against the force of the water. Brother Johann held his rope, also straining with all his might to hold both of us in place.

For the longest moment, I was adrift, like a bobbing cork, but as Percy held me I managed to touch my feet to the stream bed and then to begin pushing against the current, hoping to help the brothers drag me back. It seemed hours, though it was but a few minutes of struggle, and I began to feel the success of Percy's tugging. I was moving upstream, slowly, despite the fierce current.

At last, Percy was able to pull me close enough to shout, "Take my hand!" Johann groaned, as he strained against the rope, knowing that if Percy slipped, he could not hold both of us.

I brought one hand out of the water. Percy seized it as quickly as it broke the surface. I marveled at Percy's strength. Once he had drawn me to him, I pulled myself up to his shoulders, until my arms were around his neck. From that position, I was finally able to stand.

Percy shouted, "Hang on, Gabriel. We'll move together." From there we continued to the other side of the stream, arm-in-arm, each of us dragging our wet rucksacks in the stream, while Brother Johann reeled us in — hand-over-hand — like two big fish.

Finally, Johann gave a mighty tug. Percy fell forward and began to claw his way onto the bank, all the while pulling me by my rucksack. Then, I too fell forward onto the bank and pulled myself the rest of the way on my belly.

There I lay for some minutes, like a beached walrus, gasping for breath, exhausted from the frigid struggle. Percy and Johann did the same — wet, freezing, and with an icy mountain wind blowing across our bodies.

In what I reckoned as less than ten minutes, Brother Johann rose and hoisted his rucksack in place. "No matter that were wet," he said. "We must continue. We'll make our camp about three kilometers up the path. It's there we'll make a fire, warm ourselves, and dry our clothes."

Only one thing comforted me. I'd somehow managed to keep my spectacles. Yes, somehow. God, I supposed, had kept them wrapped around my ears.

Percy and I struggled to our feet, took up our packs, and followed Johann up the path, shivering from the mountain cold, which was now attacking us through our wet clothing. I sometimes shook so violently I feared toppling over the edge. I also worried as we climbed that our rucksacks had failed to keep our blankets and the supplies dry. All were wrapped in waxcloth against the wet, but that was sometimes insufficient to protect from a hard rain or a dousing of the kind we'd just taken.

Soon the exertion of walking helped to fight off the chill, and, in less than three hours, we entered a small glen, with a gently flowing brook and plenty of vegetation. Johann looked back. "This is it. We'll make our camp for the night here, brothers."

Johann loosened and removed Jonah's rack and then gave the donkey a ration of grain.

We immediately set about collecting fuel for a fire. When I opened and emptied my rucksack, I was relieved to see that even my bundle, which had taken a better drenching than the others, had not soaked through, and its contents were dry.

We quickly removed our clothing and wrapped ourselves in blankets, and then we arranged our trousers and tunics on rocks near the raging fire, which Brother Johann had started. As the sun disappeared and evening shadows fell over the high mountains, we fed the fire. We kept an admirable blaze a-going. Percy made a large pot of tea, and we enjoyed a meal of hard black bread, cheese, and dried figs. That and the warmth of the fire satisfied us as well as any monks could wish.

Brother Johann, who was never happier than when he was collecting and breaking firewood, went out to gather more before darkness could prevent it. Percy and I remained and continued to warm by the fire. Soon, we fell into an odd conversation.

"How did you come to the monastery?" Percy asked, out of the blue. "I mean, I know you came when you were only four years old, but how did that come about?"

"Oh, I'm not right sure. Father Abbot once told me that very likely my family were poor mountain folk. When my mother had another baby, there were probably too many mouths to feed, and so they gave me up to the monastery. That's his best guess, anyway. The brothers took me in and made a monk of me, and that's my history. I've not seen my family since, though I often wonder how they have fared and what they are like."

Percy's curiosity about my family encouraged me to ask more about him — beyond what he had told Elizabeth several days earlier.

"How about you, Percy? How did you come to work for the French? I mean, I know you became a thief, but it's a big step to... well, you know...."

"To fall in with spies? Yes, that's a story alright. I guess you could say it was an odd coincidence of sorts. There's a man in London — a big criminal by all accounts — named Otto Drummond. I learned he kept a large supply of cash and valuables in a very modern safe in his house. A very sophisticated safe. He even bragged, I heard, that his loot was secure and he had no worries because no one could open his fancy safe."

"I guess you took that as a challenge."

"Of course. You may not believe me, but I have never robbed poor and honest folk. I always looted the dishonest — like Drummond. People who are thieves, like me. Thief against thief — that's my game," he smiled. "It's far too easy to steal from honest folk. But, going up against the best in the business... well, that's a competition fit for someone like me."

"What about Mr. Drummond?"

"Oh yes. Well, I started to watch his house at night, to get an idea of his habits of coming and going, how many servants and their habits too. I hid in some hedges night after night, learning all I could about the routine of the house. Soon, I was sure that if I could get to the safe, I'd probably have half an hour to open it. I can open anything, you know. The French say I am a prodigy, rather like Mozart."

"Moz... who?"

"Never mind, Gabriel. Just never mind."

"And did you... open it, I mean?"

"Not right away. One night, as I crouched in the hedges, I suddenly felt a strong hand on my neck and then a hand across my mouth. Two men lifted me to my feet, dragged me to a waiting coach, and whisked me away."

"Oh my!"

"Yes. Frightening. The man who'd grabbed me was none other than Gérard de Montclaire. You may not have heard of him, but he's well known as a detective. But Montclaire is much more than what the world knows him to be. He's also a senior operative of the French Intelligence Service — the Deuxième Bureau — and it just so happened he'd also been watching Drummond and was also intending to loot his safe."

"Good Heavens!"

"Montclaire is bloody smart, and it didn't take him long to figure out that I might be able to open the safe, maybe even better than the seedy-looking fellow he had with him. So, we agreed to work together. At that point, I didn't have much choice."

"What happened?"

"The next night, we entered the house, when all but one servant were out. While Montclaire chloroformed the butler, I opened the safe — it was a hard one too — and we made off with sacks of banknotes and what Montclaire wanted — the records of Drummond's criminal enterprises in France.

"Well, the short of it is that Montclaire was so impressed with my work that he offered me a job with the DB, with a guarantee of good pay, as long as I gave up my freelance thievery. I did too, until I gave in to temptation and made off with that painting, right under Montclaire's nose. That really put him off. He tracked me down and caught me. Take my advice, friend. Never try to put one over on Montclaire. Well, that's how I ended up in the abbey. Montclaire sent me there for a year — 'to reflect and reform,' he said. A last chance."

2

I was about to ask Percy if he had indeed reflected and reformed when Brother Johann returned, and darkness settled over the mountains. We kept up a blazing fire, while Johann dragged up more limbs. We fed those to the fire as it burned. We said little, as we each sat on our own rock, nestled snugly in our blankets, sipping on the black tea.

Within the hour, all light had failed. Our clothes were dry, so we dressed. Wrapped in our wool coats and blankets, we arranged ourselves about the fire. Exhausted from the day's trek and work, sleep came easily, even lying on the cold rocks. Thoughts of my nice straw mattress in the Dorter floating in my mind, I soon began to drift.

It was then — in that netherworld between sleep and wakefulness — that I heard it. My heart stopped, then my breath, though at first, I thought it was a dream. A low hissing that ended in a rattling growl. Then, a stench. A putrid stink, like something dead, that seemed to follow every hissing. Percy touched my shoulder. I jumped. Johann roused himself and sat up.

"What is it?" Percy whispered.

Now fully awake, I could tell the sound came from up the path but no telling how far. I looked and saw nothing, but then the hissing grew louder and the stink more sickening. I started to retch.

"What is it?" Percy repeated, holding his blanket to his nose.

Johann stood and tossed a log on the fire. "Tatzelwurm.* For sure," he said, pulling a large knife from his tunic and looking anxiously up the path. "She won't get me without finding my knife in her neck."

I swallowed hard, my heart pounding in my chest, to think that I had now come so close to Tatzelwurm.

"What's Tatzelwurm?" Percy asked, as another, even louder hiss came rolling down the path.

Johann kept his gaze in the direction of the sound and took up his ax. It unnerved me even more to see the fear in Johann's eyes. "Tatzelwurm is Tatzelwurm, Brother. She's a creature. Lives in these mountains and she's as mean as they come. They're shy, so you almost never encounter one, but I guess we're unlucky."

"A creature?"

"Yes," I explained, realizing Percy had never heard of Tatzelwurm. "She's a d-d-dragon or big lizard of sorts, but with the head of a c-c-c-at. Never thought I'd ever encounter one," I whispered.

"I've never encountered one myself," said Johann. "But my grandmother said she came face-to-face with one once, trying to suck the milk from her cow. When I was a lad, my mother told me my uncle was eaten by Tatzelwurm. They found only his head and a few bones."

"You said she?" Percy asked.

"Aye," said Brother Johann, still gazing up the path. "All Tatzelwurms are shes. They're so mean they killed all their menfolk and ate them. That's when they started in on other animals and us humans, I guess."

We listened, as the hissing grew louder and the stink even more putrid. I vomited. We huddled closer around the fire, feeding its flames, hoping the blaze would keep Tatzelwurm at bay. The hissing grew closer, and then we heard more clearly the low growl that followed every hiss. By now, the stink was overpowering, and though we tucked our noses into our blankets, even that failed to give relief.

Dizzy, overcome with fear that Tatzelwurm would strike, dragging me off to become her evening meal, the terror seized me in its spell. I stood, threw off my blanket, and began to run down the path, away from the terrible hissing and stink. All I could think was that I must run as fast as I could, away from Tatzelwurm.

"Gabriel!" I heard Percy shout after me. "Stop!"

But there was no stopping. Driven by terror, I ran faster, until, that is, I felt something on my back, pushing me to the ground. Tatzelwurm had caught me.

I lay on the ground, my eyes closed, dreading what was about to happen, waiting to feel the first tearing bite of her teeth. But, after a moment, I opened my eyes and even in the darkness, I saw it was Percy, looking down at me.

I must have passed out at that moment, because when I awakened, Percy was shaking me.

"You might have stumbled over the precipice in the dark," he said, as I screamed and struggled to get away. "Stop, Gabriel! You'll take us both over the edge!"

"What?" I asked, as if awakening from a nightmare. "What?" I repeated, still woozy and hardly knowing what insanity my terror had made me do.

By then, Brother Johann piled on me, and between the two, I could hardly move.

"Yes," I finally said. "I won't run. I don't know what got in me. I'll stop."

Percy pulled me to my feet and dusted me off, while Johann wrapped a blanket around me. We returned to the fire and once more huddled around its warmth. The hissing continued, but now it seemed to be moving away. At least, I hoped it was.

After an hour or more, the hissing stopped abruptly. Soon, there was no more stink.

"She's gone," Johann whispered. "Might come back, but gone for now, eh?"

We sat in silence for a long while, warming by the blaze and thinking about Tatzelwurm. Then, I noticed that somehow, I guessed in my crazy flight from the monster, I had lost the silver chain and cross that I always wore about my neck — a crucifix Father Abbot had given to me when I became a monk. I treasured it, and now I was heartsick to know it was lost. "All because I'd lost my head and run," I confessed to Percy.

Sensing my sadness, Percy fell silent. Timothy sighed. I fell asleep.

3

Dawn came slowly in the mountains. I awakened before first light and lay in my blanket, listening and sniffing for any hint of Tatzelwurm. No hissing. No stink. So, I stood and began to feed the failing fire. I soon had it blazing nicely.

"We'll make the hermit's cottage by nightfall," Brother Johann said, rising from his blanket. "A good day for a trek, but the most dangerous part. The path becomes even narrower. Hugs the side of the mountain."

We trekked all day in silence, hearing only the noises of the mountains and the sound of our own breathing. As the light began to fade to dark, our path narrowed and then took us around a large boulder. Just beyond, we beheld a small rock building, with a roughly thatched roof, no larger than you would expect to stable a donkey. Just beyond, a little brook poured over the precipice.

"This is where I leave the hermit's provisions," Johann explained. "The mountain folk bring their gifts here as well — mostly small game they kill and can share. They're poor themselves, but it's God's work to support a hermit, and so they make the sacrifice. Most of them are in awe of him, but some have told me they are afraid."

"Afraid?"

"Yes. Some say he's insane. Others vow he has strange powers, and they don't want to encounter him."

"Albertus comes here to retrieve your provisions?" Percy asked.

"Oh yes... to fetch his water too, I reckon," said Johann, nodding toward the brook. "Lives up the path, I believe."

"You mean you don't see him?"

"No. I put my provisions in the little house and then go out to gather wood. I usually spend the following day cutting firewood, but after I've done that and pass another night, I leave. I've never once seen the hermit in the three years I've brought his food, but I've guessed he's seen me."

"You mean, he might be watching us now?" Percy asked, almost in a whisper. Johann nodded and then looked again up the path.

We stowed our provisions in the hut and then, as Jonah munched on some nearby vegetation, we set about collecting firewood, both to stack for the hermit and to see us through the night. Percy had not told me of the Abbot's letter, so I did not know how he would manage to see Albertus, but I knew he'd not leave without doing so. Then, he took a paper from his coat pocket and tacked it to the door of the hermit's food hut.

We worked the best part of an hour, collecting firewood. Then we moved a distance back down the path, where Johann and Percy made our fire. Before the last light, we were nestled about it, wrapped in our blankets, against the creeping chill of the night.

At first, all was silence. But then a rumble came from nowhere, shaking the ground. Instinctively, we all looked up the mountain to the west. "Look!" Johann pointed, as a boulder came hurtling through the trees and down the slope toward us. It came faster and faster, and I knew it was coming at our fire

— at us. As we all fell back, it bounced over Jonah, shot just past my head, and then bounced again over the precipice. We heard no more of it for a few seconds, until it crashed somewhere below.

We lay there a moment, breathing our sighs of relief. When we had righted ourselves and calmed our nerves, we sat once more around the fire, as the last of the day faded into a cold mountain night. A gentle but chilly breeze suddenly stirred down the slope, from where the rock had come. I don't know why I looked up the path at that moment, or why Percy and Johann did the same, but it was then I beheld the strange creature — emerging slowly, hesitantly from behind a large rock.

Jonah's ears, which usually drooped, stood up straight and tall.

Dressed all in a rough wool tunic, tied at the waist with a rope. Still half-concealed by the rock, his long, gaunt face, and piercing, fiery eyes glared menacingly at us. His white hair, plentiful and ragged, streamed in all directions from his head, as did his long, shaggy white beard. For the longest time, he stared at us, and we at him — no one uttering a word or cry.

I had seen the strange creature before. It was the angry old man I'd seen on the tower — the same who'd warned, 'Beware'.

Chapter Fourteen
Wherein We Meet Albertus

12-13 April 1911

1

He stood there for a time, half-hidden by the rock, saying nothing and peering at us with his fierce eyes. I might have taken him for a starving way-farer, except that his face was alert and somehow vigorous. Finally, he stepped out and leaning on his staff, approached slowly, hesitantly, as if he did not trust to our goodwill. He held Percy's paper in his hand.

"We're monks of Saint Ambrose," said Brother Johann.

From the time he'd begun to advance, the old man peered intently at Percy, not glancing even briefly at Johann or me.

"I know who you are," he answered. "I've seen you many times... you're the big monk who brings my provisions." He continued to look at Percy. "I have been observing you for several hours."

His voice was rough and weak, because of his great age, I thought. But then it came to me. He probably had not spoken to anyone in years and did not often use his voice, except perhaps to pray aloud. As he spoke, his voice became clearer and somehow it seemed to resonate in the mountain stillness. It was the same frightening voice I'd heard on the tower.

He came close to our fire and sat on a rock, with his hands to the flames. The fire danced high, as Johann added fuel. Across the fire and through the flames I saw those terrible eyes, still fixed on Percy. Why, I wondered, will he not take his gaze from Percy? On the tower, he had not diverted his eyes from me. I looked at Percy and saw that he was returning the hermit's gaze, apparently untroubled by the piercing stare.

We waited for Albertus to speak again, but he remained silent, warming his hands. Then, he began to look at Brother Johann and me.

"In the morning. Come up the path to my croft. Not far," he said, finally and matter-of-factly, as if he were accustomed to inviting folk to visit. "Yes," he repeated, "come in the morning."

None of us replied, though Percy nodded. The old man rose, took up his staff, and, as quick as he'd come, turned and disappeared along the path behind the big rock. We sat motionless and silent for a long while. It was as if we'd visited another world, or perhaps the distant past, where we'd been greeted by one of its lords.

"What has happened?" Brother Johann finally asked, in disbelief.

Percy answered. "Albertus may be the strangest human I've ever encountered, and I don't mind telling you, I've come face-to-face with some strange ones — bad and good. Some crazy."

"Do you mean to say...?"

"Yes," he cut me short. "We must consider that Albertus may have gone quite mad.... As some of the mountain folk claim."

"I see what you mean. Why did he look at you that way?" I turned to Percy. "Never took his eyes off you. Scary."

"Aside from wild white hair and long white beard, what did you notice about Albertus' appearance?" Percy asked.

"His eyes. They are fierce."

"Yes — and they prevent you from noticing something else."

"What?"

"His hands."

"What!"

"And his face. And his body generally."

"What do you mean, Percy?"

"Albertus is the same age as Brother Paul, right?"

"Yes. About, I guess."

"But the man we just saw is not. Oh, his white beard says so, but his hands are those of a young man. So is his vigorous body. And the skin on his face. No wrinkles around the eyes. No bags."

"Oh my, Percy. It's not Albertus then."

"No, it's Albertus all right. It's just that Albertus is not an old man. At least, his body is not as old as he is."

"And then... his eyes."

"You mean they're frightening."

"Something other."

"What?"

Percy looked at me, puzzled.

"They never blink."

We remained silent for a while because it was hard to grasp what Percy had said. Finally, I asked, "But what about his stare? Frightening."

"Didn't seem that way to me. Strange but... I didn't find it the least unsettling. No... it seemed quite natural and even a good thing, somehow.

Strange in another way too."

"How do you mean?" I asked.

Percy paused — reluctant to answer.

"His stare... it felt, like... it was a stream of energy passing through me," he said, looking into the fire.

"It's the hermit's mind interests me," said Johann. "Not being what it should. The high mountains'll do that to a man."

Percy glanced up at Johann. "Yes, and so, how will we know that whatever he tells us is not the ravings of a madman?"

No answer.

I did not say so, but all that Percy had said and what we had seen made me wonder if Albertus might not be a personification of The Evil One, and Percy somehow in his power.

The hermit's visit was hardly the strangest thing to happen that night. None of us had had a restful night since leaving our monastery, but this night, we all fell into a deep sleep within a few minutes of the hermit's departure and the next day we agreed we'd just slept the most restful sleep of our lives. I awakened to the first light over the mountain above us, and as I rose and drew in a first deep breath of the chilly mountain air, the strength of ten monks came into my body, as if I had just inhaled... well, as if I had just inhaled the energy of life itself. The first breath of life as it must feel to a newborn. Later, I found Percy already at the rekindled fire, gazing into the flames and unaware that Johann and I had taken seats on a rock beside him.

"Percy, the hermit said nothing about the book." My disappointment must have been obvious.

"Albertus knows something important about the book," he said, without looking up. "I don't know what, but he knows more about that book than anyone alive. Count on it. What I don't know is, will he tell us?"

"It looks to me a very unlikely thing that we'll learn anything about it. It's a mystery. Only Saint Hilda and God know."

He looked at me, disappointed. "Perhaps," he said. "Perhaps. Don't suppose Timothy knows anything?"

I glanced about and saw Timothy, standing by the big rock, his arms crossed and his eyes tossed up toward Heaven.

"No," I reported.

"I hope you'll forgive me, Brother Gabriel, but that guardian angel of yours seems a real underachiever. You were issued one of the early models."

I did not reply. I heard Timothy sniff.

We packed our blankets and gear, and Brother Johann led the way around the large rock and up the path to where Albertus had told us we'd find his cottage. Soon, a little rock building, nestled into the side of the mountain, with a rough shake roof, came into sight, high above the path. We climbed a gentle slope for about ten minutes to reach the hermit's camp. As we looked out on the broad expanse of the valley far below, I knew we'd found a place so lonely that only eagles and hermits dared to perch upon it.

2

Albertus stood at the door of his hut, staff in hand, again peering sternly down at Percy. In the night, I had figured out why he looked so intently at Percy. The hermit somehow knew that Percy is a thief and is generally unrepentant about it, and so his stare is the fierce gaze of God's reproach. On the tower, it now seemed to me, he must have wished to remind me to beware of Percy's sinfulness? Now, he means to strike the fear of eternal damnation into Percy's black heart, I figured, so as to bring out the good in him.

Finally, we reached the croft, which was not much larger than the storage hut below. We remained silent, waiting for Albertus to speak. He motioned us to come sit round his fire, which was raging in a big circle of rocks just out front. The ground surrounding the rock cottage was clean and everything, including the stack of firewood just outside the door, seemed neat and tidy. Plenty of time to tend to such things, I thought, when you are a hermit.

We sat on logs arranged around the fire. Big logs — too big for one man to drag into place, but somehow Albertus clearly had. The hermit offered each of us a tin cup of his strong black tea. We shared cheese and black bread from our rucksacks. We sat in silence, enjoying our meal and sometimes looking out from the hermit's croft to the wondrous sight of clouds drifting through the valley below us.

Then, Albertus spoke in a clear and melodic voice. "I have known that something strange must happen because I have seen it in my mediations. A premonition, you might say. For the longest time, I could not imagine why, and God did not give me to understand my quandary. It has troubled my waking hours and even my dreams for more than a month."

He looked into his cup and sipped his tea. "Every day," he continued, "at least once, there has come the same thought into my mind, as if a voice from somewhere — someone — speaking to me in a whisper. And the voice says only this — 'He comes.'

"And now, this letter from Father Abbot explains everything. It's you who has come, and it's the book you wish to know about. Saint Hilda's book."

"Yes," said Percy. "Does that surprise you?"

"No. I thought it might be that... the book. For me, it always seems to be that book."

"You are here because of that book. Is that not so? It's why you choose the life of a hermit, eh?"

Albertus looked up, surprised.

"Yes," he said, then peered into his cup again. "Very perceptive of you to imagine that." Before Percy could continue, Albertus stood, his face as fierce as ever. His eyes hard. "What is your name?" he asked.

"Percy. I am a lay-brother of the abbey. This is my friend, Brother Gabriel. Our friend Johann is also a lay-brother."

"You speak Latin well. Where did you learn it?"

"From my father. He was a scholar — also an Anglican vicar. We spoke it together."

"I see." He paused. "He taught you well.

"I will speak to you alone, Brother Percy. Come into my house."

3

Brother Johann and I could not hear what was said when Percy and the old man disappeared into the croft, but Percy told me much of it later. Albertus offered him a chair in the dim room, by a small hearth. The hermit sat in another. He looked at Percy earnestly, leaning forward. But Percy spoke first, continuing his questions.

"The book in the Scholarium was stolen, but the thief died — apparently — and the book has been returned. Brother Paul told me that you and he had studied it together and found it difficult," Percy explained.

The hermit's eyes softened. "Brother Paul... how is my old friend?"

"He's well," Percy lied, not wishing to distress the hermit. "He's had a bit of trouble lately, but will recover nicely."

"Good," the hermit said, as he smiled kindly. "Brother Paul is a fine man, and I have often missed him."

"And your studies together? You have missed that also?"

"That book in the Scholarium," Albertus scoffed, his face once more fierce. "That book is a fraud... a mere copy. I studied it enough to know that. And it's not even complete. Whoever copied the original — and that is what I concluded eventually — whoever did that, made a poor job of it. It's a fragment at best and a poor copy in the bargain."

"But it is old."

"Oh, yes. Very."

"You came here — became a hermit — because of the book? How did the book send you here... to be alone?"

"Saint Hilda's book is bound to be the focus of evil and violence, Brother Percy, because of what it is. I'm not surprised someone has died. I fled from it. It's no fault of the Saint... it is the fault of the book, and whoever wrote it. It has the power of great good, I believe, but it is bound to be the focus of evil and of evil men. I could see that when I read what it aimed to tell."

Percy perked up. "And what was that?" he asked, leaning in and sitting on the edge of his chair.

"Full of incantations and formulae, that's what. God help me, it seemed that the Saint's book is almost certainly a satanic thing." He shook his head and bowed.

"Why do you say that?"

"I was able to decipher many of the strange words. One word that appears over and over set my very soul on edge."

"What word was that?"

"Ahriman,*" he said, trembling and then shaking his head.

"What?"

"Ahriman!" He shuddered, as he said it again. "Not what, but who. Ahriman is the Zoroastrian spirit of Evil and Destruction. The Prince of Darkness himself — that's who he is! Well, that was enough to turn me away from the book... and... and to bring me here."

"What was said about him? Ahriman?" Percy asked.

"Ah... that is apparently the purpose of the book, but I could discern very little beyond that. I could only make out a vague assertion that the book conveys... and these are the very words... Ahriman's most alluring promise to mankind. Yes, those were the precise words. Satan's greatest temptation to man is in that book, and when I saw that I wanted to have nothing to do with it.... never have it in my hand again. It's an evil thing," he whispered, as if conveying a secret. "The book promises something that all men want, but only at the price of worshiping Ahriman."

"But surely you have thought about it? Have puzzled what that promise is? Surely," Percy pressed.

The old man's eyes grew sad. He looked at his hands. "Oh yes. I have considered, and I believe I know. That thing that would be 'most alluring.' Something so desirable that some men would worship the Evil One to have it."

"What is it?" Percy asked.

"Let me ask you, Brother. What is it that most men wish for — even more than the hope of salvation and paradise?"

Percy paused. Then suddenly his eyes grew wide, but he was speechless.

"You needn't say it. It's enough I see you know. Yes, that's what the book conveys."

Albertus closed his eyes. "Yes, and it is a profane promise. Profane," he repeated. "I concluded Saint Hilda must have brought the book to the monastery to hide it and keep it out of reach of mankind. To save the world from it. But it torments me to question why she did not destroy the evil thing." He shook his head.

"Yes, I see," said Percy, who by now could see the old man was tired. He paused to give him time to recover.

Now, the hermit's eyes filled with anguish. "Enough talk of the book, Brother Percy. No more. No more for now."

Percy was full of questions and one in particular, but he had no choice but to hold them, in hope of a chance to ask later. Albertus walked to the corner of his hovel, knelt on a flat stone, and began to mumble his prayers before a rough-made cross on the wall. Percy rejoined Brother Johann and me, and we decided it would be best to use our time to gather firewood for the hermit. Someone had given Albertus an old bowsaw and ax, which we used to make kindling of the limbs we'd managed to drag in.

The day passed in just this way and the toil of making fire logs tired all of us. Brother Johann finally called a stop to our work just as the hermit emerged and sat with us by the fire. We warmed our hands, and Percy spoke.

"But then where is the book, Brother Albertus? The first book I mean, the one from which the copy was made? What has happened to it?"

At first, the hermit's eyes flashed — even angrier — at the question. He stood and looked into the fire.

"Alas, Brother Percy, I don't know. And, I know I cannot persuade you to abandon your search for it."

Percy looked down, disappointment in his face. Albertus continued.

"That voice. The one that said, 'He comes'."

"Yes?" Percy asked.

"I knew who it was."

"Who?"

"The Saint... she told me."

"Told you what?"

"A vision — in a vision. A dreamlike vision. Just over there," he said and nodded, "near that rock. Saint Hilda herself came to me. All aglow she was. At first, I fell back, blinded by the sight of her... and afraid."

"And?" asked Percy, only half believing. He later told me that he suspected the old man was surely insane — a sad result of his lonely life.

"She said...." He stopped, as if to collect his wits, or perhaps to relive the emotion of the moment. "She said, 'You must tell him. Tell him to look to our beloved Ambrose. Look to him. Tell him that, Albertus. Ambrose will guide him.' At the time, I didn't know what to make of it... what she was telling me to do. 'Tell who?' I asked her, but she said no more and then faded away. I was left blind the whole of that day and night. I lay in my cot, thinking I would never see again, but also wondering what the saint had meant by her strange instruction."

"I see what you mean," said Percy, still doubting.

"And now I know," he smiled faintly. "Now I know. It was you who was coming, and it is you the Saint wanted me to tell. 'Tell him,' she said. You are 'him,' Brother Percy."

He paused a moment, regaining strength.

"I can tell you this. In your quest — whatever questions you have — do as the Saint says. Look always to Saint Ambrose to guide you, because it is there you'll find your answers. He looked into the fire and repeated, "Oh yes... your answers are there. The Saint says so."

Still seeming tired, the old man looked earnestly and even sympathetically at Percy. "You wish to know where to find *The Chronicle of Secrets*? I do not know where it is, Brother, and I dearly hope Saint Ambrose will guide you away from it."

I might have expected Percy's eyes to fill with disappointment, but instead, he smiled faintly.

Then Albertus began to drift, his eyes dreamy. Percy thought he might be falling asleep, except that then his eyes opened and grew fiery once more. "Be afraid, Brother Percy! Fear that book! There is great danger for you — or anyone — in such knowledge. Do not be tempted by it, I beg you!"

When Albertus had said this last, his body lost all strength and then slumped, as if relieved of a great burden.

We helped Albertus into his croft and left him in his cot, mumbling his prayers. We all slept soundly by a blazing fire that night. The next morning, we shared our provisions with the hermit. As we prepared to leave, Albertus said this one last thing.

"You'll face even greater danger on your return, so I bid you be constantly on your guard. A great Evil is stocking you. And you, Brother Percy, your danger is greater still, but if you are able to return to the abbey, give this letter to Father Abbot, along with my blessing." He handed Percy a sealed paper, and then we knelt to receive the hermit's blessing.

When I looked up, I saw that Albertus' hand was outstretched toward me, and in it the silver cross I had lost.

"Here, Young Brother. This is yours," he said, in the same tone as the old man on the tower had said 'Beware.'

I gasped, and my mouth fell open with joy, as I took it and put it once again about my neck.

When we had walked some ways down the path and approached the big rock, I turned to look back. There I saw Albertus, standing above, his staff in hand, the rising sun behind him, and for the slightest moment, I thought I saw Our Lord, transfigured. I turned away, lest I should not see such a thing. I did not look back.

Chapter Fifteen

Wherein We Are Deceived
by the Demons

Good Friday, 1911

1

We descended all that day, using leg muscles we'd not needed on the climb. We rested often. Retracing our path seemed at first much easier than our coming. Faster too. For one thing, we'd all loaded our rucksacks on Jonah. And the path was now familiar and downhill. Always downhill. Still, we learned that the descent could be as treacherous as the climb because it was even easier to lose footing and slide.

I was much relieved when we passed the place where we had encountered Tatzelwurm. Still, I worried some about the creature as we camped that night. Happily, the stinking creature did not trouble us. Next morning, as Johann loaded Jonah, I asked, "Will we make the abbey by nightfall?"

"We may expect to arrive by Compline, Brother, if it's God's will," he smiled.

That last bothered me a little, because I have learned in my fourteen years that God, though admirable in every way, is distressingly unpredictable. I do not know why He is that way, because it is disturbing, and Timothy has never answered my questions on the issue, but there it is. We marched on, happily, with confirmation from the expert mountaineer.

Later still, when we approached the rushing stream, where I had almost drowned, the sound of the raging water seized me with fear. Percy must have read the fright in my face.

"Easy, Gabriel. You're an expert at fording this stream by now."

He was right. I made it with no difficulty at all, and I was delighted to think myself a better mountaineer.

The terrain became a little flatter as we descended, and we were able to pick up our pace. Well, Brother Johann set a faster pace for Percy and me, and we kept up. Clearly, Johann was pressing to make good his predicted arrival by 6 o'clock. I was reassured that we each of us carried a small torch, in case we were forced to walk at night.

Our trek proved slower than Brother Johann had predicted, and it was mainly because of me. I stumbled so often that Johann slowed our pace. When I finally fell, I cut my knees and forearm, and it took more time to bandage my wounds.

It was growing late as we came down from the mountains and into the valley. As we reached the wagon trace, I looked out to the great distance and my heart leapt with joy to see it. Though we were still far away, the abbey stood high on its mountain, shining in the last glow of sunlight.

Once in the valley, our path took us past scattered cottages and meadows. Johann picked up the pace on the level terrain, still determined to make good his prediction we'd reach the abbey by Compline. A disturbing thought came to me. We still had to pass through the Forest of Ohme, and now we would inevitably do so at dusk — that time of day when even the saintliest monk would dread to pass through a thicket of demons. I was sure that Percy and Johann were thinking the same thing, and yet the big monk pressed on faster than ever.

"Have you ever found yourself in the Forest of Ohme at night?" I shouted ahead to Brother Johann.

"Yes," he answered, grimly.

I waited for him to say more, but more never came.

"Did you find yourself confronted by demons, then?"

No answer.

"By that, I mean did you see anything?"

"Yes, Brother. I did," he said, still grim.

All this left me free to assume that we would have the worst of it from the demons, as we dared to pass through their domain at night. Prayer became my constant relief, as we reached the trees and the trace led us into the dense forest.

2

In the vast forest canopy, what remained of the evening light faded quickly into darkness. The air itself thickened and filled with unusual smells that I had not noticed when we passed before, during the day. When all light had faded, Brother Johann stopped, opened his rucksack, and drew out a small torch, which he lit. Percy and I did the same — the first time on our journey we had needed to use them. The torches lit the path for only a few meters around us, but in the dreadful darkness of the forest, we welcomed even a little light.

Less than an hour in, we found ourselves surrounded by flickering lights, which flitted about our heads. It was a wondrous sight, as hundreds of the little lights danced about the forest, some a few feet off the ground, and others high up in the canopy. We stopped and looked all around us, amazed at the show of lights.

"What is it, Johann? Have you ever seen this?" I asked.

No answer.

"What is it?" I repeated.

After a long silence, the big monk spoke. "Yes, I've seen 'em. Once before."

"What are they?" asked Percy, wide-eyed, his mouth open.

"The mountain folk say they're the souls of them that have been taken by demons, as they passed through the forest. Souls captured and not set free to go to Heaven is what they say."

We moved faster, and at first, the little lights followed us, but then they fell behind. Almost immediately, as we walked, we heard a chorus of evil voices, chanting a hellish song — as dark a melody as I'd ever heard — a song, I presumed, the souls in hell must be forced to sing in praise to Satan.

The voices followed us a full kilometer into the forest and then, suddenly there arose out of the doleful chorus a single voice — a woman's voice in song. An angelic voice, it seemed to me — growing louder and louder still. As I looked about, wondering where the beautiful voice was coming from, I noticed that Percy and Johann were also looking side-to-side. Now, for the first time, someone besides me could hear the voices.

Then, the voice also stopped, and in the unnatural silence that followed, we heard quite a different sound on the road ahead of us — a clattering of sorts and then the whinny of a pony. We could see nothing ahead in the darkness, but shortly there came into the glow of our torches a cart, driven by an old woman, with a young girl at her side, and pulled by a pony that seemed ready for the grave. The old woman and the girl looked frightened, and I could see the girl had a bandage on her forearm. I breathed my relief that the noise was harmless.

"Good evening," Johann greeted. "We are monks of the abbey, returning from a journey."

The old woman and girl pulled up, and I could see that immediately the fright disappeared from both faces.

"Good evening to you, Brothers," she said. "A dreadful thing to be in the Forest of Demons at night."

"What puts you here this time of day?" Johann asked.

"We're just come from Chaumont," she said. "The girl 'ere cut her arm this morning, as you can see, and we made for the doctor in the village. We're frightened to pass the forest at night, Brothers. Would you see us to the end, in the name of God? Have pity on us, Brothers."

The woman looked wretched, the girl terrified. Both dirty, thin, and frightened of the forest demons. Their trembling reminded me of Elsie.

"Yes," said Percy, "we'll see you to the valley." My heart sank.

So we turned and led the old woman and her cart, retracing our steps, lighting the way with our torches. Only now, I noticed that the little lights were gone — where once they'd danced around our heads and in the trees. So were the singing voices.

As we walked, we heard only the constant clop-clop of the pony and clatter of the old woman's wagon behind us. Finally, when we neared the edge of the forest, we stood to one side and turned to let her pass, only now we could see to our fright that she was not there. We heard still the noise of her wagon, getting louder and louder, as if passing us, but there was no cart, no pony, no child, and no old woman. Just the sound of their passing. Then, the old woman began to laugh — a cackling rejoicing — and the girl squealed with laughter too.

I saw Percy and Johann looking to one side and another, as if expecting to be attacked. Then, the sounds faded, as if the cart had passed on its way to who-knew-where, and the hideous laughing died away. When there was no noise at all, we stood motionless, looking at each other and mystified.

"Hurry!" Johann finally shouted. "For some reason, the demons wanted to slow us. I cannot imagine what they have in store for us if we are in the forest at midnight. When their power is greatest."

As we began to run, the chorus of evil voices resumed, only now behind us — pursuing us. The hideous chant grew closer and louder as we ran, and somehow — I don't know how — I knew they must not overtake us. That whatever the demons had in store for us, it would surely overwhelm us with their chant.

The chorus of the damned thundered in my ears, with deafening intensity, but still, I ran after Percy and Johann, with all my strength and all my wind.

Sometimes, we seemed to be outdistancing the terrible voices, but when we stopped to regain our wind, they came rushing on, louder than before.

At last, our dead run spilled us out of the forest and onto the road to Austria, where I fell onto the gravel and dirt. The voices came on, but when they reached the forest's edge, they quickly weakened and faded to silence.

We lay on the road for some time, breathless and exhausted, like rodents who'd been run down by a rapidly-moving coach. When I opened my eyes and looked up, I saw Timothy, sitting on a large rock, looking down at me and shaking his head.

What's the matter, I thought.

"All that running and flailing about has ruined my new walking shoes. That's what's the matter," he said. "And look here — a tear in my new breeches," he whined.

Just as I was about to sympathize, I heard Johann's voice, urging us forward.

"The hour's already well past Compline Brothers. We must be on our way."

On the road, Johann soon broke into a joyous hymn, and as we sang, I rejoiced to think we'd outrun the demons and their satanic chant.

We scrambled up the road at the double-quick, with more energy than I thought I had left in my legs. In the hour it took us to reach Chaumont, our torches began to dim. Before they failed entirely, however, we came in sight of the stone bridge and soon stood before the great gates of the monastery. Never was I happier to read those words of our dear Saint Ambrose above the gate. Never, as we knelt to give our thanks to God for his protection during our journey, was I happier to hear the gate creaking open on its rusted hinges.

Chapter Sixteen

Wherein Percy Makes a Fateful Decision

15 April 1911

Old Brother Valerian, the gatekeeper, hardly knew what to make of us, but he quickly recognized our voices and opened wide. Brother Felix in the Refectory gave us food and drink, and in the half-hour's time, we made our way to the Dorter and our cells, where I collapsed onto my blessed straw mattress.

I had no consciousness of the ringing bell for Matins, but I jolted to Percy's hand on my shoulder, shaking me from a deep sleep. "Up Gabriel. Get up. It's already Matins."

We struggled to change our dress, splashed cold water in our faces, and then followed the brothers down the nightstairs to the chapel. Father Abbot smiled to see us enter and take our seats at the end of the row, alongside Brother Johann. "Greetings," he said, "to our three brothers, who have returned. Praise God for their safe journey."

Beside Father Abbot, Prior Oswald sat with his glum face, which was now mostly clear of the horrible affliction God had given him. I am sure the monks were whispering that Saint Hilda had finally answered their prayers and had forgiven him for doubting her tears.

After Matins, Percy handed the hermit's letter to Father Abbot, who smiled to receive it. Just as I was thinking how sweet it would be to return to the Dorter for more sleep, Percy stopped me short of the nightstairs, in a corner of the Cloister.

"In there, Gabriel... just now... I became sure of something the hermit only hinted to me," he said, in an excited whisper.

"Oh? What's that?"

"No time now. In the morning will be time enough. Now's time for more sleep, and we will need it."

That last, ominous advice bounced around in my head as I lay back down to sleep, and it kept me awake longer than I wished.

2

That morning, at the Guest House, as Percy and I moved about on our knees, scrubbing floors, I suddenly noticed a dress and a crutch standing beside me.

"Elizabeth!" I heard Percy say, as we looked up.

The French girl hovered, arms crossed, looking down at us. "You're back," she said, with no particular glee. We both stood.

"Yes, and I might as well tell you, our visit to the hermit was successful."

"Oh?" she questioned, clearly hoping to hear something interesting. So was I.

"Yes. It was a great deal of bother, but I learned precisely what I'd hoped. At least, I think I did. The hermit talked in riddles, but... well... I know what I know."

Bother? Bother! I thought to myself. My knees are shredded from tumbling down the mountain. I almost lose my life at every turn of the path, and he calls it a 'bother'? We were chased the length of the Forest of Ohme by a pack of murderous demons and he calls it 'bother'? Near tragedy, I call it.

"So, the hermit knew more about the book, as you suspected?"

"Well, yes. You might say. He confirmed that the book in the Scholarium is but a poor and confused copy of an original."

"My papa knew that much. You didn't have to climb the mountains to discover that," she scoffed.

Percy continued, undisturbed. "Albertus also told me a great deal that he had learned and had surmised about the original book — its purpose — but he couldn't tell me where it is."

"Percy," I intervened, "why do you bother so much about the original book? It's probably lost. In any event, why does it matter? Why not leave it be? Let the lost remain lost, because it's probably God's will that it should be."

I didn't tell Percy, but in my secret thoughts, I still feared he was so determined because he meant to make off with the book. So, I only half-believed his answer.

"Listen, Gabriel. I got dragged into this book business because someone took it, and everyone suspected me. Father Enrico was probably in league with whoever took it. I believe that person pushed him over the Precipice and tossed the copy over with him. I don't doubt there are some — Prior Oswald, for one — who might just think that I pushed Father Enrico."

"Threw the copy away? But why?" Elizabeth asked.

"Because that person figured out the same thing we have... that the copy is a worthless fragment. And, he also figured what I did. If there is a copy...."

"...There's an original. And where is the original?" Elizabeth finished the thought, smiling smugly.

"Give the lady a prize for two correct guesses," said Percy. "Assuming that someone killed Father Enrico and disposed of the copy — probably to call off the search for it and him — and made the murder look like an accident, then that someone is probably still here — and is still looking for the book. And that someone might be clever enough to find it."

"But why murder Father Enrico?" Elizabeth asked.

"Hard to know. Maybe he got cold feet when they discovered the stolen book was useless. Rather than let him run for it, maybe his partner killed him and used Father Enrico's death to throw everyone off his scent."

"Everyone but you," said Elizabeth.

Then Percy turned again to me. "And that, Gabriel, is why I am bothering about the original."

"And you want to beat the killer to it, eh?" Elizabeth asked, her eyes wide.

"Percy! You won't steal it to sell, will you?" I asked.

"No. I won't."

"What then?"

"I want to settle a score with the loathsome son-of-a-something-or-other who made it seem that I'd taken the thing. That really puts me off. Under normal circumstances, I might enjoy the challenge of finding the book, which would be nice and maybe even profitable. But now, I just want to nail that person. If I find the book and turn it over to Father Abbot, that person's plans are ruined."

"You thought it was my papa," Elizabeth said, frowning.

"Yes. For a brief moment, but not any longer. You must admit, he fits the bill." Percy challenged, "but you convinced me he's not the one. But then, who is?"

"Who?" Elizabeth asked. "Did Albertus tell you?"

"No. He couldn't even tell me where the book is hidden. At least, not in any direct way. He talked mostly in riddles and visions — imaginings and mediations. He even has visions — maybe hallucinations — of Saint Hilda. Still, he told me something just as good."

"Really?" I gasped. "What? And where?"

"In some things he said, and in what he says Saint Hilda told him, there is a faint hint of what I most want to know."

"And you have thought of it, have you? Teased out the meaning of that hint?" I asked. "I know!" It suddenly dawned on me. "Prior Oswald. He's had it all along, eh?"

Percy looked at me blankly.

"It is where it has always remained hidden, except for that time when someone tried to make a copy of it. Where it belongs."

"Where, Percy?" Elizabeth insisted.

"In the crypt with Saint Hilda, of course. It's her Book and she guards it. Or, rather, the same force that guards her tomb also guards the book, don't you see?"

"Holy Mother of God, Percy! You cannot mean to break into the crypt!" I protested, stunned.

"Shush!" he said, his finger to his lips. "You'll tell the whole Guest House."

"But... but..." I stammered.

"To answer your question," he whispered, in a calm voice. "That's exactly what we are going to do... and we'll do it tonight."

Elizabeth's face lit up, while I remained speechless at the sacrilege Percy was planning. She is a sinful girl, who suits Percy's even more sinful personality perfectly. Together, they are a whirlwind of sinful inclinations, and that, of course, is just the kind of situation where God's word is needed most.

Elizabeth took Percy's hand, her eyes focused in a grave expression. "I don't know how you plan to do it, Percy," she said, "but you can count on me. I'm with you." She smiled faintly.

"We? W-W-We are going to break into the S-S-Saint's crypt? Tonight? You are including m-m-me in this great sin you are proposing?" I asked, turning to Percy.

"Listen, Gabriel. I'll explain. *The Chronicle of Secrets* belonged to the Saint, and it was once available for the monks to study and perhaps even to present to the world for its betterment. Albertus says it must be the focus of evil, but how can we be sure of that? Perhaps the book was so special to Saint Hilda because it could bring good to all God's people? In any case, it is a great possession of the abbey, and it is now lost, or at least, missing. I believe it got locked away in that tomb — perhaps to safeguard it — but who would ever give us permission to unlock the crypt to find it? I'll answer that for you. No one. But just think. Maybe the book is meant to be known to the world, and somehow God's will is being prevented by it being locked away all these years? How are we to know?

"Albertus says the Saint appeared to him, right? Maybe he was hallucinating.... I don't know, but he says she told him about me."

"You're right, Percy," Elizabeth chimed in. "And how is anyone to know, if they cannot read the book?" She stood up to her full height and gave me that look of hers that somehow always reminded me of Prior Oswald.

"Very well, Gabriel. I'll make you a bargain," Percy continued. "If we find *The Chronicle of Secrets*, we'll leave it up to Father Abbot what to do with it. It'll be his decision, and I know you'll trust him to do the right thing."

Elizabeth raised her eyebrows and gave me that withering look again.

I thought for a long moment. The two of them were getting impatient with me. Elizabeth crossed her arms and started tapping her good foot. She frowned down on me too, which was disconcerting. Then, I looked around for Timothy. He was standing to one side, with his arms crossed too, only he had the faintest smile on his face. Then, he did the unexpected. He nodded, "Yes."

"Very well," I said, exhausted and half-astonished that I'd been talked into invading the Saint's tomb.

"Excellent," Percy smiled. "You'll be pleased you helped, and when the entire monastery celebrates the recovery of the book, you'll be a hero, Gabriel."

3

Percy's logic appealed to me. If the hermit hinted the book was in the Saint's tomb, and if Saint Hilda meant for the world to know — for its betterment — how could I stand in the way of that?

"Why not just tell Father Abbot about your suspicions, and let him decide to open the crypt?" I asked.

"Simply this. Someone here is a murderer, and the book is somehow at the bottom of that murder. If I tell Father Abbot what I suspect, how are we to know it won't get to the killer? Someone in Father Abbot's trust, maybe. No. Better to tell no one until we're sure we can lay our hands on the book."

"When do we go, and how will we open the crypt?" Elizabeth asked, her voice and face full of excitement.

Percy looked at her a long moment. "You're not going in the crypt, Elizabeth. You are going to be our lookout."

She frowned and crossed her arms again. A bad sign. I winced and then braced for the return of the angry French girl.

"We need you to warn us if we are to be interrupted," Percy explained.

"And how am I going to do that?"

"The Guest House stands between the abbey and the crypt, and the pathway runs past it. You'll be able to see anyone who is on that path after we reach the crypt. If you see someone, ring the Guest House bell. We'll hear it in the crypt, and we'll clear out before that person arrives. No one would be surprised to see you at the Guest House. But if Gabriel were to be seen there, at that time of night, it would be sure to arouse suspicion."

"But, if I ring that bell, it'll rouse everyone," she protested.

"No matter," Percy said. "The more confusion you cause, the better for us to escape."

I could tell Elizabeth didn't much like the lookout job, but no one could say it wasn't important to have such warning. Her face relaxed. "Oh, very well."

"Gabriel and I will wait until just before midnight, so you must be on your watch before then — 11 o'clock. You'll see us go past soon after. Understand?"

"Of course, I understand. D'you think I'm a half-wit? Doesn't take much brainpower to keep watch."

"No. It takes good eyes and staying awake. Think you can manage that?"

"Yes." She frowned.

"Very well, but you're forgetting one thing," I spoke up. "The mysterious force. The force that guards the crypt. That high iron fence is there for a reason — to keep people like us safe from the force."

"I know," said Percy, and then he swallowed hard.

Chapter Seventeen

Wherein Percy Fails

15 April 1911

1

I doubted Percy's prediction about being the abbey's hero. Instead, all afternoon, as we worked at our Guest House chores and then reported to help in the Refectory, I had visions of myself being dragged off by Captain Ulrich — to prison. I sighed, often.

The hour before midnight came too soon for me. Percy and I took to our cots after Compline with our clothes on, and at eleven o'clock we crept unnoticed past the cells of the brothers, down the nightstairs, and into the Cloister. Soon, we were on the path to the Guest House, trusting — but not certain — that Elizabeth was already on watch and could see us pass.

Down the hill, about fifty meters, stood the Saint's tomb, surrounded by the abbey's cemetery and the tall iron fence, with spiked finials at the top. Once at the great iron gate, with its large, forbidding lock, we dared not light a candle. Working only by moonlight, Percy took from his pouch some small tools such as I'd never seen, and somehow he felt his way to opening the lock. In less than a minute, I heard a clanking sound, and the big lock fell open. Percy pushed the gate slowly on its rusty hinges so that their creaking was a low groan rather than a shrill scream. The sound made me think once again of the dreadful force. We entered and closed the gate behind us.

A few meters in, we stood at the tomb's great iron door. It looked like the door of a treasure house, with its iron straps, giant hinges, and rivets all over.

"No!" I said, driven by a sudden impulse of fear and conscience. "We must not touch it, Percy. Let's go. The mysterious force will surely strike us dead, as soon as you touch the tomb."

Percy's jaw stiffened, and he looked at me a long while. "Gabriel, maybe you're right, but we've come too far to stop now. Stand back."

2

My heart stopped as Percy felt his way to the lock. Now he worked in a way I could not see, for more than five minutes. All that, while I prayed thanksgiving that the guardian force had not yet struck us dead. I heard Timothy mutter, "Don't know why or how. The Saint must approve of Percy, for some strange reason."

Percy groaned.

"What is it?" I asked.

At first, there was no answer, but then another clanking sound. "Voilà," said Percy, once again opening the door slowly, painfully, on its groaning hinges. We walked in, closing the door behind us. As Percy lit a candle, we beheld the full horror of what stood before us. Another great iron door, even uglier than the first.

"What is that?" I asked, to no reply.

This door was different — like no other I'd ever seen. First, it had no lock and no hinges, at least none I could see. To the left side of the door, also on an iron wall, there were two vertical rows of large… well, I can only call them iron buttons — each button about five centimeters in diameter.

Percy inspected them, tracing up and down with his candle, not knowing himself what they were or even what to make of the strange door. On an impulse, I reached out to touch one of the buttons.

"No!" he shouted in a whisper. "Don't touch it!"

"Why not?" I asked. "What are they?"

No answer. Instead, Percy continued to stare at the buttons, still moving his candle up and down the vertical rows. It seemed to me he was counting them, but I did not hear him do so. When he spoke, what he said shook me to my sandals.

3

"We can't open this door. We dare not even touch it."

"What?" I whispered. "We can't get in? Not even try?"

"No. Let's go. I'll explain later."

Percy blew out his candle. We retraced our steps, closing first the tomb door, then the gate, and then made our way quietly up the path, past the Guest House, and into the Cloister. Once there, I took Percy's forearm. "Why did we fail to open the crypt? What was that door? And those strange buttons?"

"That crypt is not a tomb. It's a safe, and that door is the door to an odd kind of vault. Like in a bank, only much older and cruder. But it's no less tricky. Those buttons on the side — the two rows?"

"Yes. What are they?"

"They're a cipher of some kind. If you push them in a certain order, each will operate a separate lever inside the panel and the proper sequence will finally trip the door's latch. Like tumblers in a modern combination lock, eh?"

"Good God in Heaven! Percy. How will we ever know how to work the cipher?

He gazed at me with an odd look in his eyes. Strange as it was to see it in Percy St.-John's face, it was the look of defeat.

Chapter Eighteen

Wherein Elizabeth Challenges Percy

Easter Sunday. 1911

1

When we answered the bell for Matins, I could see that Percy had not slept, and his face was drawn with worry. Afterward, we returned to the Dorter, and I asked about what I suspected — that our failure at the crypt was tormenting him.

"I've thought and thought about that cipher, Gabriel, and it's just too complicated. There are so many buttons and so many possibilities," he said, shaking his head. "It's the cleverest puzzle I've ever seen. How can I know what it is? It could be anything! An Abbot's name or the name of his mother. Anything. It might even be random things, which only the inventor knew by memory. Do the buttons stand for letters or numbers? Or, one row of each? How should I know?" He shrugged.

Percy seemed utterly lost — unsure of anything and even beginning to doubt himself. "Maybe, Percy." I tried to comfort. "Maybe it's God's will that the tomb must remain closed and, if *The Chronicle of Secrets* is there, that it should remain out of reach. Even Timothy says so."

He looked at me in his sympathetic way. "If that is so, Gabriel, then I have no further business here, and I can do the abbey no good by recovering its precious book."

"At least, we will have the satisfaction of knowing that whoever killed Father Enrico — if indeed he was murdered — cannot have the book either," I assured.

"Not necessarily. Consider this. What if the book is not in there? Does that mean the murderer has found it and now it is gone from the abbey forever? If it's in there, maybe the murderer is cleverer than I am and can get to it?"

When I returned to my cell to sleep, I tossed from one side to the other, worrying about Percy. I liked the idea of giving up and leaving the book and its secrets to God and Saint Hilda. I did not like the sad effect that defeat was having on my friend, but I rejoiced secretly that Percy could not now be tempted to steal the book, as I still suspected in my deepest heart.

The next morning, when it was time to report to the Guest House for chores, I could not find Percy. Not in the Refectory, nor the Locutory. Finally, I stopped Brother Felix, who was walking up from the Baking House. "Have you seen Brother Percy, by chance?"

"Why, yes," he replied, looking back. "Not five minutes ago. On the path to Precipice."

2

To hear that Percy was at the Precipice, and in his despairing mood, frightened me. I hurried down the path toward the Guest House, thinking to turn off from there to the Precipice and to find Percy. But almost as soon as I took the path, I met Elizabeth.

"What's the trouble, Gabriel? You're in a frightful hurry about something."

I explained to her quickly about Percy's mood the night before. I told her all we'd learned, especially about the cipher, and then told what Brother Felix had said... about seeing Percy down at the Precipice. Elizabeth looked out to her left, and so did I, but there was no sign of Percy.

"Let me go with you," she urged.

I agreed, and we struck out, crutch and all, across the uneven terrain toward the Precipice. We walked down well past the Stables and Baking House before we finally spotted Percy, standing on the edge, looking out toward the mountains. He was so preoccupied, he didn't notice our approach until we stood behind him.

"Don't!" Elizabeth exclaimed. "Don't jump, Percy! Please!" she pleaded.

Percy turned around quickly, startled.

"Jump? Me?" he said, and then he burst out laughing.

"Stop laughing at me. I was only concerned for you," she scolded, a little embarrassed at showing her emotions. "Gabriel told me you were here. He also said you are melancholy."

"Yes, I suppose I am. I'm stumped... defeated by that bloody cipher. Guess Gabriel told you about that too? But you needn't worry about me — jumping. I've been in tighter spots than this."

"Very well."

"Still, I hate it. That terrible cipher may be the one puzzle that even I can't solve. That's what distresses me. It's my trade, you see, to solve those things, and... well, how can I claim to be the best at my trade, when I've crashed at the ripe old age of fifteen? I mean, what's left? I'll be forced to consider an honest occupation. Perhaps even go to university and become a professor, or worse, a lawyer."

"I don't believe you've failed, Percy," said Elizabeth. "You can defeat the cipher. Papa says you are a genius at such things. He's even heard of you, though he says they are not good things to hear, and he heard you were arrested. I don't know. I've never seen you open anything, but I believe in you. Just so you know that. I believe you can darn well do anything you want to do, including defeating that cipher."

Percy smiled at Elizabeth's confidence.

"However," she said, frowning and crossing her arms, "if you are more content to wallow in uncertainty than to spend your valuable time thinking up a solution... down here feeling pity for yourself, while that puzzle is waiting to be solved...."

"It's not true, Elizabeth. I'm not spending my time feeling self-pity. Well, not entirely. I came here also to think of a solution, but every time I come up against it, nothing comes to mind."

"Well, at least now we know the mysterious force that guards the crypt. It's the force of that awful cipher," I said.

"Exactly. Whoever invented that thing endowed it with almost supernatural powers to protect the crypt, even from someone like me."

"Did the hermit know anything of it? Did Albertus mention it at all, even in a vague way?" Elizabeth asked.

"No. He said nothing about a cipher, certainly."

"Then, what did he tell you? Anything!"

"Now that I think of it, Albertus seemed most eager to tell me about his strange vision of Saint Hilda, and what she had said... what she had told him to tell me."

"What?"

"That I should look to Ambrose, whatever that means. I can't see how that...."

3

Percy stopped in mid-sentence, his face frozen, eyes wide. Speechless, and staring blankly toward the mountains.

"I guess you're right. That doesn't say much.... What is it, Percy? What's the matter?" Elizabeth asked when she finally noticed Percy's strange trance.

Elizabeth and I looked around, but we saw nothing. "Percy," she repeated. "What is it?" She shook him by the shoulders. Then took his hand.

He turned and looked blankly in Elizabeth's eyes, then smiled.

"Percy St.-John, you stop smiling at me in that idiotic way, and tell me what you're thinking," said Elizabeth.

"Elizabeth," he gasped. "I've got it. Gabriel, I've got it! I mean, there's nothing certain, mind you, but I just know it. And yet I cannot prove it." Then, he started to jump up and down and dance about like a lunatic, singing "I've got it... I've got it... I've got it...."

All this shocked me and frightened Elizabeth, and I did not like the sound of that phrase 'dead sure.' "What are you sure of?" she asked, confused.

"I'm sure that good Saint Ambrose is the key to that cipher."

"What! Percy, start making sense, or I'm going to fetch Papa and Father Abbot. You're sounding crazy. Looking crazy too."

"Elizabeth," he said, earnestly, taking her by both arms. "Trust me. I'm not crazy."

Percy turned again to me, just as I was thinking something like, 'Uh, I'm not so sure'

"I know it!" he said, excitedly. "Gabriel, I know the cipher!"

I was stunned. Elizabeth shouted, "Hurrah! Hurrah! Oh, Percy!" And we all began to dance in a circle, shouting "Hurrah!" All of us, as crazy as Percy.

I heard Timothy say, "Good Heavens!"

Chapter Nineteen

Wherein Percy Decides

Easter Sunday. 1911.

1

As we celebrated Percy's breakthrough, it dawned on me that I was cheering yet another excuse for doing dangerous and questionable things. I was soon shaken into my senses, when I heard Timothy say, in his sarcastic way, "Ask him what he has in mind."

"What is it?" Elizabeth insisted, as we stopped dancing. "I want to know."

"Never mind that," said Percy, "the important thing is we must go back to the crypt tonight."

"You see," I heard Timothy say, clicking his tongue.

"Oh no!" I exclaimed, mostly to myself and with no confidence my objections would stop Percy.

"But you must tell us," Elizabeth continued. "I won't help unless I know." She folded her arms and stiffened her neck. "Me neither," I said.

Percy's eyes relented. "Very well. The first thing to consider is that that door and cipher are about as old as the tomb itself. Very old. Right? And whoever made it had a devilish mind. A truly diabolical mind. I know, because I have one of those myself."

I was just thinking that Percy had that one right, and more's the pity, when I heard Timothy say, "He's not lying about that!"

"What do you mean?" Elizabeth asked.

"I mean the cipher is made to open the door only on a set sequence, and if one error is made, the cipher will reset to random, and the door will be impossible to open."

"Oh my," I remember saying.

"Yes. That was clear to me last night, and that's why I told you not to touch it, Gabriel. One wrong button and the cipher self-destructs. That's what's so devilish about the thing. It's unforgiving, and it will punish a wrong guess. One wrong button — we've lost."

"So that's why you stopped me touching it. I'm happy you did."

"Sadly, there's no knowing for sure what the cipher is, without knowing from the person who made it, and that information is not retrievable. So that requires us to make the best guess possible. It must be an inspired guess, however. I have put my imagination together with all that Albertus said. Now, I am prepared to take a chance."

"Why? What is your inspired guess?" Elizabeth demanded.

"Without knowing it — or maybe he did — the hermit told me. They are the very words he says the Saint conveyed to him."

"What words?" I asked, now confused again.

"He said to look to Saint Ambrose to know the answer to mysteries. Well, the mystery of that damnable cipher, I believe, is in the words of Saint Ambrose."

"I'm lost again, Percy," I said.

"So am I... I think," Elizabeth agreed, frowning.

"Gabriel, what is the one thing about Saint Ambrose that every monk who has ever lived at this abbey since its founding has known? Even the illiterates who cannot read or speak Latin know it. What?"

I thought for a moment, and then it came to me. "It's the inscription! *Veni Redemptor Gentium*. 'Oh Come, Redeemer of the Earth.' Everyone knows that."

"Yes! Don't you see? That must be it. At least, of all the guesses we can make, that's the best one by far. And there's something else."

"What?"

"How many letters are there in the Latin alphabet?"

Even I knew that, but before I could answer, Elizabeth said, "Twenty-three. The Romans didn't have the K, Y, and Z, except when they wrote Greek words."

"Exactly. And guess how many buttons there are."

"Twenty-three?" I guessed.

"Yes... and that's one indication that whatever that cipher is, it's in Latin."

"That's a pretty thin reason for supposing the cipher is the inscription, but you're right, Percy. That is the best guess," Elizabeth reasoned.

Percy's face grew dark. "Yes," he repeated, "the best guess... but maybe wrong."

2

We turned and walked up toward the Guest House. When we reached the path, Elizabeth stopped and turned. "I want to go this time. You're going tonight, and I want to go."

"No. It's too dangerous. After all, there's probably a murderer about, and besides, we still need you to keep a lookout, in case we're followed."

"Too dangerous? Since when are you allowed to say what's too dangerous for me? Let Gabriel keep watch, while I go with you. I deserve my chance," she insisted.

"Yes," I said, eager to remain as far from the crypt as possible. "Elizabeth deserves her chance."

Percy shot me one of those glances that conveyed six or seven of his favorite curses, but then his eyes softened. "Very well, Elizabeth. Gabriel will keep watch. I'll come at midnight. Don't be late."

Elizabeth smiled and walked away. "Don't be late," she scoffed.

3

Once we entered the Cloister, Percy had become thoughtful again — silent and brooding about something.

"You've grown quiet again, Percy. You're having second thoughts about making another attempt on the crypt, aren't you?"

At first, he didn't answer. Instead, he just looked at me with a strangely distant expression in his eyes.

"No. Not that."

"What then? It must be something."

"Yes. Something I've been thinking about since we left the hermit. I was thinking about it too, just now — down at the Precipice."

"Must be important then."

Percy sat down on one of the stone benches that the pilgrims often use. I sat beside him.

"It's all about what I'm going to do from here. About everything that brought me here in the first place, and everything I'm going to do after."

"You mean about your future?"

"Exactly. The point of the thing was that I'm supposed to reflect. Well, at first I thought that was a bunch of bunk, and I only went along with it because I had to. And at first, this place gave me an epic case of the willies, I don't mind telling you."

"I'm not sure I know what you mean, but very well. What's different now?"

"I guess this business of the book started to focus my mind, but it was meeting Albertus that's caused me to decide. There was something in Albertus — his voice maybe — that reminded me of... that reminded me of my father. Guess it was that, more than anything, that caused me to decide."

"Decide what?"

He looked at me again, and this time his eyes had resumed their usual fierceness.

"Decide to do the right thing — the thing my father would be proud to see. Decide that if I ever get myself out of this bloody mess, I'm going make a commitment to the French and stick with it. I'm going to give up my freelance thievery and throw in with the Deuxième Bureau. That's what."

He shook his head and set his jaw when he said those last two words.

"I believe you've certainly decided for the best, Percy," I told him, as happily as I could, while thinking to myself that I had hoped he would decide, somehow, to remain at the abbey, as a lay-brother. I don't think he heard me, because then he repeated — blankly and mainly to himself — "If I ever get out of this."

Chapter Twenty
Wherein Percy Proves His Genius

Midnight, Easter Monday, 1911

1

Once again, as we had the night before, Percy and I rose just before midnight and slipped down the nightstairs. This night, however, there was an unexpected difference. A great storm had come down from the north, such that any noise of our going was more than covered by the thunder that rumbled through the caverns of the abbey.

"Gabriel," Percy said, taking me aside to one corner of the Cloister. "I've been thinking. It will be best for you to take up your watch from here, where you can see the path to the Guest House and beyond, to the crypt. You'll be able to see anyone who follows us or who goes down to the crypt after us. If you see such a person, you'll know what to do."

"What?" I asked.

Percy looked at me, his eyes full of pity.

"Warn us, of course. Run to the Guest House and ring the bell. Ring it like your life depends on it."

The coward in me still rejoiced at being left behind.

"Rely on me, Percy. I'll watch closely."

Lightning illuminated Percy's way from the Cloister, and by the time he reached the Guest House, he was soaked. He found Elizabeth crouched in the entrance and swaddled in a blanket. For some reason, she was trembling, and in the next flash of lightning, Percy could see her face was full of terror.

"What is it?" Percy asked, fearing something had gone terribly wrong. Perhaps with her parents.

At first, she said nothing but continued to shake in stunned silence. Percy asked again, peering closer into her face and taking her by the shoulders.

"The storm," she said, her voice trembling. "I'm deathly afraid of storms. Always have been. It's horrid."

Percy saw immediately the need to change plans. "Can you watch the path and warn me if anyone comes? Follows me?"

"Yes, I think so," she said, softly. But then, she seemed to awaken from her fear. "No!" she insisted in a whisper. "I'll go. I'm going!"

Percy took Elizabeth's hand and, at first, had to pull her from the doorway. But then she moved on her own, struggling on her crutch and still holding his hand, sometimes squeezing it. They struck out for the crypt, each step illuminated by a new flash of lightning. Each time the lightning struck, Elizabeth jumped, but the two continued down the path, hand-in-hand, until they stood before the iron gate.

By now, the storm was so thick I couldn't see the entire path from the Cloister, so reluctantly I moved down to the Guest House, where I took up my watch in the shelter of a side door. From there my view of things was much better.

At the gate, Percy made easy work of the first lock, as he had the night before, though in the storm he was a bit slower with his little tools. At the iron door to the crypt, he once again defeated the old lock. The door creaked open, and there, just inside, stood the amazing iron door with its buttons.

Elizabeth told me later all that happened in the crypt. She and Percy lit their candles, and as they held them high, Percy took another long look at the vault door and sighed. He stood in awe of the thing, convinced he'd broken its secret but still not sure.

He closed his eyes for a long moment, while Elizabeth looked on. I like to think he was saying a prayer, but Timothy says probably not.

"Here, take my candle," he said.

"How do you know which buttons are which letters?"

"Like French and English, written Latin is a left-to-right language, so I assume the top button on the left row is 'A'."

Elizabeth nodded, but unsure. "Wait, she said," always full of questions. "The inscription has some letters twice. What do we do there?"

"Once a button is pushed, you cannot push it a second time, I must suppose," Percy explained.

"Yes, and...?"

"This is tricky. My assumption is that once a button or letter is pushed, it also is pushed for the second and subsequent occurrences of that letter. In the inscription, the V, I, M, N, R, and T are used twice, and the letter E is used four times. Some letters are only used once and some not at all, of course."

"Percy, that's a big assumption."

"Yes. I know. But it's necessary if you believe the prayer from Saint Ambrose is the cipher."

Percy took a deep breath and looked at Elizabeth. Then closed his eyes again. She smiled and touched his hand. Then, he began to push the buttons. "V first, and then E," he said, making sure to push the buttons in those positions, from top to bottom, as Elizabeth held high her candles. "N and I."

"I just thought of something," she said.

"What?"

Lightning suddenly hit nearby the crypt, followed by a deafening clap of thunder. Elizabeth jolted, then shuddered.

"Should you skip a space? And how would you do that?" she asked.

"No space. By the twelfth century, it's true, Latin had acquired spaces between words, but the Latin that Saint Ambrose wrote had not yet done so. Therefore, no spaces needed."

Elizabeth smiled and nodded, as Percy continued to push buttons, making sure to count properly so as to push the buttons in the right order. After each push, they heard a metallic click. Finally, when he'd finished the inscription, he nervously took hold of the door's handle.

"Moment of truth," Elizabeth sighed, as Percy and she looked at each other.

Percy pulled. Nothing. He pulled harder, and this time the door seemed to move. "It's rusted shut. Help me pull," he said. Elizabeth put aside the candles and both took hold of the handle. The ancient hinges creaked and groaned, but finally the door moved a half meter open.

Elizabeth smiled. "Percy, you're a genius."

"You doubted it?"

"Yes. To tell the truth. I did. I thought you were mostly English bluster."

Percy shook his head and clicked his tongue. "Sad. Very sad."

"Don't you tut-tut me," she said. "Just open the damn door."

Candles held high, they peered into the darkness. "Oh no!" she gasped. "Another door!"

3

There, before them, less than two meters into the tomb, stood yet another iron door, this one with a small, barred window in it. Percy inspected it quickly. "No problem here," he concluded. "This one's just a locked door."

Again using his small tools, he began to work the lock, as Elizabeth lit his way. He looked up in frustration.

"What's wrong?"

"The old tumblers are rusted. Can't move them."

Then, Percy drew from his marsupium a small leather pouch, opened it, and sucked its contents into his mouth. Then, putting his mouth to the lock, he blew the contents of his mouth into it.

"Yuck! What's that?" Elizabeth asked, a disgusted look on her face. "Excuse me. I'm going to retch."

"Butter. Melted butter," he replied, and then returned to his work. Finally, in less than a minute, Elizabeth heard something click.

Percy looked up and smiled. "Open," he said. The door opened a little by pulling, so the two pulled harder, once again fighting against rusty hinges that squeaked and squealed, as if feeling the pain of being forced to work after centuries of sleep.

When the door was finally open, Elizabeth held high her candle and gasped — then screamed, as lightning suddenly illuminated the room. There, on a high table before them, lay the skeleton of the Saint, her hair, long and white, still streaming from her skull, and her arms crossed upon her chest.

"Look!" Percy exclaimed. "Look. In her arms, resting on her chest. The book!"

Elizabeth's eyes opened even wider, and she let out a little squeal. "Oh, Percy. It is. It's *The Chronicle of Secrets*."

The two stood in dumb silence beside the saint's skeleton, gazing upon the strange apparition before them, only half believing what they could see.

"Well, well," said a familiar, smiling voice from behind them. "You've done well, Brother Percy."

Chapter Twenty-One

Wherein We Come Face-to-Face

With the Murderer

1

The two spun round, Elizabeth holding her candle high. They could see only a small shadow standing in the doorway.

"Sister Rose. Come in," said Percy, in a strangely off-handed way. "I've been expecting you."

Thunder boomed outside, and a flash of lightning illuminated the Irish nun's face. It also showed the pistol in her hand. Sister Fiona stood beside her, also holding a pistol.

"Expecting me?" Sister Rose asked.

"You gave yourself away some time ago, Mr. — ?"

The old nun's mouth dropped open a little.

"Tandy. Mr. Tandy's m' name," he said, taking off his nun's vail. "How'd I give m'self away, exactly, if I might be so bold as to ask? I thought I did my Sister Rose character pretty well."

"Nothing wrong with your playacting, Tandy. It's your Irish."

"Irish? But I am Irish, you English bastard," he protested.

"Yes, but it's clear you know too little of Ireland. If you did, you'd know that there have been no wolves in Ireland for over a hundred years. No, you might have been born in Ireland, but you've never lived there. America?" Percy asked. "And then, there's the matter of your fork."

"My fork?"

"Yes. I noticed you hold it in your right hand. Americans use the fork in the right hand. The Irish hold it in the left — same as we English bastards."

"Quite so," said Mr. Tandy, his eyes now changed from smiling to cold. "Quite so, clever boy. Aye, my saintly parents took me from Ireland as a babe, don't you know. But you're not clever enough to keep me from that book, eh? You made a mistake in leaving the outer gate open for me. Tut-tut. Now, I'll be havin' that book, if you please. Girl," he motioned to Elizabeth, "take it from the saint and give it to Fiona here. The Saint'll not be needin' it now, and I have a great need of it, don't you know." He smiled in his sinister way.

As he motioned Elizabeth with his pistol, there came another flash of lightning and clap of thunder. "Be quick, girl. No time to waste," he scolded, now frowning. Elizabeth moved to do as she was told, but just then came a loud clanking sound from outside. Mr. Tandy's eyes goggled, then filled with fear. Percy smiled.

2

"Mr. Tandy. You have the pistol, but I have you," said Percy. "That sound you heard was exactly what you thought it was — 'Twas the outer gate locking. I'll thank you to hand me your pistol — slowly."

"Aye, lad. You're a clever boy. It's that damn dull-witted friend of yours, eh? When I saw you come down the path alone, I figured you'd left him behind. And when you and the girl went to the crypt alone, we followed, thinking the stupid monk had run out on ye."

"Brother Gabriel is not dull-witted, Mr. Tandy. He knew to hide himself until you showed yourself, and then, as you've now seen, he also knows how to lock a gate," Percy smiled.

Just then, Tandy sprang toward Elizabeth, seizing her by the hair, pulling her into his arms, and putting the pistol to her head. Elizabeth screamed in pain. Percy winced, as he heard the click of the pistol's hammer. Tandy smiled. Fiona pointed her pistol at Elizabeth and cocked it.

"You out there, lad," Tandy shouted to me. "I have the French girl by the hair and a pistol at her head. Open that gate, boy, or I'll shoot her, sure as you're a dimwit of a monk."

For a moment my brain went blank, and my eyes stopped seeing. I was overcome by fear and had no notion of what to do. All I could think was that Elizabeth was sure to die if I did not do as Tandy said. I had locked the gate, but there was no way I could do as he demanded. He clearly thought I had a key, but I did not. Percy knew it too. If Percy had wanted the gate open, he would have opened it himself, I figured. So, it seemed to me that Percy's silence was telling me what to do.

"Well, what'll it be, boy? We don't have all night. This girl's about to die."

My heart stopped. I couldn't breathe — like when I was under water in the stream and drowning. Then, I heard a voice, and I turned with a start. It was Timothy. When I faced him, he said nothing, and then he did the strangest thing. He just smiled at me, confidently, and somehow that relaxed my entire body. I could breathe. Then, still silent, he did something even stranger. He shook his head, slowly. I knew in an instant what he was telling me to say.

"No, Mr. Tandy. I won't open the gate. You'll just have to shoot the French girl. But if you do, you and Sister Fiona will surely go to the guillotine, whereas now you'll merely go to prison. It's your decision, not mine."

Tandy's face suddenly turned white. Percy knew Elizabeth would die in the next second and that he would follow soon after.

"What if I shoot the girl? Then you get to decide if your friend, Brother Percy, gets to be next, eh? What do you say to that?"

"I am sure that Elizabeth will be with God in Heaven today," I said, "and that is surely the goal of every Christian."

Tandy closed his eyes. "Goddamn, that monk! Just, God damn him, and all like him!" he shouted. "I should have known he'd be unreasonable. His kind always is."

"Well, there you have it, Tandy," Percy decided to say, his heart pounding. "That's what you get for trying to bully a dull-witted monk. It's like trying to intimidate a turnip. Just doesn't work."

It was then Fiona lowered her pistol, turned, and walked toward the crypt door. I saw her as she emerged, but it was not Sister Fiona. It was the woman in the red scarf. The woman who had left me at the monastery gate and who had said, "I love you." As she approached me, she seemed to glow gently in the darkness.

"Gabriel," she said softly, "you must save your friends and open the gate. Please, Gabriel, do as I ask," she pleaded, her arms outstretched.

My heart melted at her plea, but then — I don't know why — I knew the woman could not be real. That it was somehow a trick.

"No," I said, "I won't open it."

At that, the woman in the red scarf began to melt into a snarling doglike creature, hissing and spitting at me. A demon. But instead of fright, I was strangely calm and confident that as long as the demon was locked in the Saint's tomb, it could not hurt me. The Saint would protect me.

"No!" I said even louder. "I won't open the gate. Never!"

The snarling devil dog turned again into Sister Fiona, and then she turned calmly and walked toward the tomb.

When Fiona returned to Mr. Tandy's side, he relaxed, and, letting go of Elizabeth, he lowered his pistol. "You're right, goddamn all monks! The bastards just don't see things clearly, do they?"

"Afraid not," said Percy. "That's why they're monks, after all. Just not fit for the real world. Like you and me."

Tandy shook his head in pity and disappointment.

"Time to give me the pistol, Tandy. So that you and Fiona will be safe from the likes of Brother Gabriel. He — and that pistol — are likely as not to get you killed."

Tandy shrugged. "Aye, you're right there, lad," he admitted, handing Percy the pistol. Elizabeth took Fiona's pistol and moved to Percy's side.

"Gabriel, are you still there?" Percy shouted.

"Yes, Percy," I replied. "And I am n-n-not dull-witted, M-M-Mr. Tandy. I am as witted as anyone."

Elizabeth moved to go but then saw Percy staring at the book for some reason. He stepped beside the skeleton and then reached out to take the book from Hilda's arms.

"No, Percy!" Elizabeth insisted. "You must not take it."

Percy looked at her. "That book is £50,000 to me, and a ticket to safety."

Elizabeth gave him a withering look but said nothing.

"But you're right. I must not. I've made my decision and I'll stick to that."

Elizabeth smiled, as Percy took her hand. The two moved carefully past Tandy and Fiona, who turned to watch them back through the door. Percy quickly pushed the interior door shut, and the lock clanked, as the tumbler fell once more into place. Tandy peered through the barred window, his little eyes wide.

3

"But what's this, lad? You'll not leave us here, eh? And what about the book?"

Percy smiled. "Mr. Tandy, that's exactly what I intend to do. To leave you and Fiona. And the book? Well, it's of no further interest to me, now I've found it. I know it's safe. Besides, the hermit told me to fear the book, and so I think I'll take his warning and leave it where it is."

Tandy's eyes bulged. "But... We'll die in here. You must come back to release us. Get Father Abbot, eh? Please!"

"Not sure I can do that, Mr. Tandy. You'll understand. And if you get bored, just read the book. Interesting reading, they say."

Tandy and Fiona began to scream and shriek in horror to the sound of thunder outside. Percy closed the outer door, and, as all its tumblers fell once more into place, only the noise of the storm remained.

"You're not going to leave them in there, surely," said Elizabeth.

Percy smiled his evil smile, but said nothing.

Chapter Twenty-Two
Wherein Percy Explains

1

Percy picked the gate lock from the backside, once again in the rain, and he did so with such ease that it seemed like magic. By now the storm had become a driving rain. We scurried up the path to the Guest House.

"Tomorrow," Elizabeth said to Percy, as he opened the locked door.

"Yes. Be at the Locutory after Prime. And, bring your parents. That's when... well, that's when." He shook his head.

"Right," she smiled and then closed the door.

In a few minutes, Percy and I had climbed the nightstairs and were in our cots, pretending to be asleep when the bell sounded for Matins. As we took our seats in the chapel, I thought Father Abbot looked at us strangely, but Percy assured me later that it was just my guilty heart.

When Matins ended and we had returned to our beds, I slept the sleep of the saved. Such a sound sleep, in fact, that Percy had to rouse me when the bell sounded for Lauds at 5 o'clock. This time, I was sure that both Father Abbot and Prior Oswald were looking at me strangely — not just a fit of guilt. I wondered what could be the matter. I discovered when the office was ended. Father Abbot stepped from his chair at the head of the chapel and said, "Brothers, something disturbing has happened. Brother Jean-Baptist, the rector of our Guest House, informs me that two of our pilgrims went missing, sometime in the night. Sister Rose and Sister Fiona cannot be found, and we fear the worst. It's far too dark and the storms too fierce for us to search for them now, and we dare not go down to the Precipice, but we will organize an effort in the morning, after Prime."

I thought Percy might speak up and settle the concern, but he remained silent and Father Abbot dismissed us to our early morning chores. Meanwhile, the storm continued to rage outside, as Percy and I went with others to clean the Refectory, before breakfast. Just after Prime, we returned with the brothers to the Locutory to await the bell for breakfast. There we found Elizabeth, her parents, and several of the other pilgrims, Mr. Covington and Mr. Westerman among them. Father Abbot usually came late, but today Prior Oswald was early. When the Abbot arrived, Percy stood suddenly.

2

"May I speak, Father Abbot?" he asked, bowing his head and in a tone that was unusually meek for Percy. At first, Father Abbot was a little startled, but then he nodded, and so Percy looked around. Elizabeth stood by her papa, peering intently at Percy, with a look on her face like she'd just swallowed a frog.

Percy launched right into his story, giving all the details. How he had determined to find the book. How he'd discovered that the book in the Scholarium was a worthless copy and only a fragment. Monsieur Dugard backed him on that. Elizabeth smiled.

Percy told how he had never believed that Father Enrico's death was an accident. How he had concluded it was murder, that Father Enrico was probably not even a priest, and that there must be an accomplice, still in the abbey.

When he said all that, the monks began to murmur to each other. Prior Oswald scoffed. But none of that stopped Percy. He pressed on with his story.

He told how the copy only encouraged him to want to know where the original was to be found and more — what it had to say that made it so valuable. That someone would kill to get it.

Percy looked for some reason at Mr. Westerman, who stood next to Prior Oswald. He seemed to me to smirk, for some reason.

Percy also told how he'd figured out that only the hermit, Albertus, could have those answers, and how Albertus added to what he knew.

"What!" Prior Oswald shouted. "How did Albertus do that?"

"Albertus encouraged me to imagine what he suspected, and I did. You see, Albertus is intelligent enough to know the power of imagination.

"And what was that?" Prior Oswald huffed. "What did you imagine?" It seemed to me that Prior Oswald had asked like a person who had no imagination at all.

"I imagined what I dared not even say out loud."

"What?"

Percy looked around, then down.

"The book — *The Chronicle of Secrets* — Saint Hilda's book — conveys..." Percy paused in mid-sentence, almost as if he were still afraid to say it.

"*The Chronicle of Secrets*... conveys the Secret of Eternal Life."

At first, there was only stunned silence. Then even louder murmuring. Someone blurted, "No!" I heard Prior Oswald shout, "Blasphemy!"

"Albertus is one of those people who are intuitive in the extreme. Talking to such people excites the imagination, and that's what happened to me. My imaginings soon turned into convictions, and by the time we'd returned from the hermitage, I knew what I must do."

"What?" asked Prior Oswald, still in a red-faced huff.

Percy drew a deep breath. "Enter the Saint's crypt."

There was a collective gasp. Someone shouted, "Sacrilege!"

Now, Percy told how he had unlocked the tomb, found the strange door, with its devilish cipher. The mysterious force, which guarded the Saint's crypt. He explained how, with the hermit's help, he had broken the cipher and how he and Elizabeth had finally opened the tomb and found *The Chronicle of Secrets*.

Elizabeth peered out from behind her papa and said, "Yes we did." Her mama gasped.

And last, Percy told of our dreadful encounter with the murderer and how I'd saved him and Elizabeth. The monks looked at me strangely. Prior Oswald frowned and then demanded: "Who is this murderer then?

"The murderer is Sister Rose," said Percy, "and she was assisted by Sister Fiona."

"The missing pilgrims?" Monsieur Dugard asked, surprised.

"Sister Rose is not missing, Monsieur. You'll find her and Sister Fiona locked in the crypt, with the book," Percy explained.

"And, he's not a nun! He's a man!" Elizabeth added. "His name is Mr. Tandy."

There were cries of surprise and more long murmuring. Father Abbot spoke next, and he seemed strangely calm.

"What Brother Percy tells is a revelation. You startle us, Brother. Please, all of you return to your work and prayer, while I speak with Brother Percy alone."

3

When they were alone, Abbot Bartholomew told things that Percy had only suspected.

"I knew of the cipher, Brother Percy, but was not at liberty to tell anyone of it. Abbots of Saint Ambrose have all known of it, though it did none of us any good. So, I considered it to be merely a quaint thing."

"I don't understand," Percy said.

"Yes, well... in the past the abbots knew how to work the cipher. I knew that from the records of my predecessors — former abbots, you see."

Percy looked puzzled.

"But then, the knowledge of the cipher was lost, in 1762, when Abbot Peter died suddenly, without passing the cipher on to his successor. His successor decided that rather than attempt to work it, he should assume that the Saint wished it to remain unknown. And so, we abbots have been content to leave it as it is. A mystery.

"Still, I confess I did not know of the book — Albertus never told me his suspicions — and I never suspected it was in the crypt."

"Well," Percy said, "you're free to leave it now, though that may be a bit of a hardship on Sister Rose and Sister Fiona... er... Mr. Tandy, I mean."

"Then, I suppose you best tell me the cipher, so we can release Mr. Tandy — to a proper prison," said the Abbot.

Percy told Abbot Bartholomew the cipher. He smiled to hear it.

Wherein My Life Is Changed Forever

1

The next day, as Percy and I took up our work at the Guest House, we learned that several of the pilgrims were preparing to leave, among them Elizabeth and her parents. I was sad to know that Elizabeth would go, but Percy seemed more than sad—he fell into one of his brooding moods.

By afternoon, many of the pilgrims had assembled in the forecourt, where Father Abbot and all the monks had gathered to wish them God's grace and a safe journey. Percy and I stood among the monks, to one side. I saw Elizabeth begin to look about, as if searching for something — or someone. Finally, she spied Percy and came over to where we stood.

Taking up Percy's hand, she said, "Good-bye Brother Percy. I will miss you. You too, Brother Gabriel, she said and kissed my cheek. "I don't know that I have ever known anyone like you, Percy St.-John."

Percy looked at his sandals. "Thank you, Elizabeth. You are special too. Very much so."

"I did not get my miracle," she said, smiling faintly and holding up her crutch.

"Miracles come in all shapes and sizes." Percy frowned. "Keep up those hopes, and it will happen," he added, with real conviction.

"No worry," she said. "I'm fine. When I came here, I wasn't. I was angry about it and thinking it would always keep me from doing what I wanted... what I needed to do."

"Oh?"

"But now, I know I can do most anything, and it was you who helped me see that, Percy."

Elizabeth had begun to cry. Tears streaming on both cheeks. I was tearing up too.

"Now that we must say goodbye, will I ever see you again?" she asked, sadly.

"Adieu, Elizabeth. I will see you in Paris, within the year. I promise."

She smiled broadly, threw her arms about Percy's neck and kissed him on the cheek. And then, I am scandalized to say, on the lips.

"Adieu, Percy," she said, as she turned and walked toward her papa.

2

The next day, Captain Ulrich arrived, and without delay, he and his policemen accompanied Father Abbot to the crypt. Percy and I were not asked to come, so we watched the goings-on from the Guest House terrace. When they had opened the crypt, they found Tandy and Fiona. They also found that Mr. Tandy had gone raving mad. Several policemen soon dragged the two from the tomb, squinting and disoriented, their eyes blinded by the bright sun. We could hear Mr. Tandy shouting a multitude of Irish curses, damning Percy St.-John to hell for locking him in the crypt.

As they dragged Mr. Tandy and Fiona past the Guest House, Percy smiled and waved his goodbye. Tandy spit and cursed at him, promising revenge. As he did so, I could see that Mr. Tandy was frothing at the mouth, like the rabid wolf.

Captain Ulrich moved to put his prisoner in shackles, but just then Mr. Tandy bolted and dashed down the path toward the Precipice. Ulrich and the policemen hurried after him, and we followed at a sprint.

At last, we caught up with Tandy, as he stood facing us, his back to the edge of the Precipice. We all stopped short.

"Tandy," the Abbot said. "Come down from there."

Mr. Tandy's placid face gave way to a faint smile, as he said, "My hearty thanks to all of you for coming today. To bid me farewell. Good-bye, dear friends!"

And then, to our horror, he closed his eyes, laughed, and fell backward over the Precipice.

Later, the monks said it was surely Saint Hilda who had stricken Mr. Tandy with the madness, but I knew the true reason he'd gone frothing mad. I had figured it out the night before. I knew then, at the crypt, that Fiona was Satan himself. Ahriman, Percy called him, but still the Devil. And it was spending the night in that crypt with Ahriman that had driven Tandy insane. Maybe Satan took his revenge on him because he had failed to escape with the book? Several days later, we heard that somehow on the way to prison Sister Fiona had managed to escape. Disappeared.

3

In the weeks that followed, Percy continued his year at the abbey, and we both celebrated that our days were once again dull and peaceful. The abbot permitted Percy to resume his studies in the Scholarium, though Percy told me he had no wish to examine further the book that had caused his troubles in the first place. Nor did he wish to read *The Chronicle of Secrets*, which Father Abbot decided to leave with the Saint.

Then, one day in mid-summer, a strange young man arrived in the forecourt, mounted on a great dapple grey horse. He wore a brown riding-habit, shiny black boots, and a long silk scarf about his neck. Percy and I watched his approach from the parapet of the church's tower, and, as he dismounted, I asked, "Who could that be?"

I was not expecting Percy to answer, so it surprised me to hear him say, "That, dear Gabriel, is Adrien Sax. One of the most artful blood-spillers you'll ever want to know."

"Who?" I asked, my mouth agog.

"An agent of the Deuxième Bureau. They call him 'Le Médecin' because he's a medical doctor by training, but an intelligence officer by trade, and a very good one too. His colleagues have a grim joke about him."

"What?"

"They say he's the only doctor in France who still practices blood-letting."

I did not find that the least humorous and I told Percy so.

"Yes. I suppose you have to be in that business to appreciate the humor," he allowed.

"But why is he here?" I wondered aloud.

Percy looked at me, his eyes sad. "Only one reason, Gabriel. He's come for me. I had thought the French would leave me here until November, to finish my year in the abbey, but..." He shrugged. "Apparently, something has changed their minds."

It came as a sudden shock to me that Percy would be leaving. Somehow, I'd never thought much about it, even though I knew the day would come. My head filled with all sorts of thoughts and emotions. It was like a panic... like someone was about to die.

In less than an hour, as we continued our work sweeping the Cloister, Father Abbot summoned Percy to his room. Percy put his broom aside and looked at me.

"Brother Gabriel, I've given it some thought during the past hour, and I've wondered about it even before."

"Yes." I followed. "What's that?"

"Come with me to Paris. To the Deuxième Bureau. I've solved the problem of the book, so I doubt the French will jail me, or even hold a grudge. Be my colleague and my trusted ally, and I will see that you are well-paid for your work."

I was dumbstruck by the notion — and confused. Not knowing what to say, I protested, "But Percy, I'm... I'm a monk. The monastery is the place for a monk. I... I... I don't know," I stammered.

"There are monasteries in Paris, Gabriel. You can be a monk wherever you go. I will arrange it that Father Abbot gives you a leave-of-absence, so you can return any time you wish. Come, Gabriel," he said with a smile and a kind of joyous excitement. "Come with me, and be a monk in Paris. I need your help."

I thought for a long minute, turning over everything I could think. My head swirled. Dazed. I thought too how wonderful it had been to see the world on our journey to find Albertus. Then, surprising myself, I said, "Very well, Percy. I'll go. If Father Abbot allows it."

"Did Timothy tell you to say 'yes'?"

I looked around and saw Timothy standing in the corner of the Cloister, his arms folded and his eyes gazing upward. Strange to see it, but he was wearing a beret.

"Yes!" I said. "He says 'Yes'!"

When Percy entered the Abbott's study, he found Adrien Sax standing by the small window. Tall and handsome, with lustrous black hair and a thin mustache, he smiled.

"Bonjour, Percy," he greeted, enthusiastically. "I've come to fetch you home, to the Deuxième Bureau. Our employers have some work for you to do. Abbot Bartholomew has given his blessing. Be prepared to travel by morning."

Percy nodded, and then he thanked Father Abbot heartily for all his care and hospitality.

"Percy St.-John," the Abbot replied, "the pleasure was entirely ours. You have given greater service to this abbey than we can repay. You've restored our most sacred relic to us, and you have been a good and faithful brother, even when others — myself included — were making it almost impossible for you. I offer you my thanks and my blessing, Brother Percy."

It was then Percy broached the plan that I should accompany him for a leave of absence from Saint Ambrose. The Abbot was taken aback but then relaxed and smiled.

"I suppose, if that is what Brother Gabriel wishes, I must agree. And I do. In fact, I agree heartily, with only one proviso, which I will impose on Brother Gabriel"

"What is that?" Percy asked.

"He must maintain his discipline as a Benedictine monk, including his tonsure, and he must report to me every month his experiences in the world. And, he must serve at our Benedictine abbey in Paris.

Percy agreed.

"You are a thief and a naturally sinful person, Brother Percy," Father Abbot continued. "But Monsieur de Montclaire and Dr. Sax here have explained that your great genius for... for acquiring things can be turned to good purpose." He threw his eyes heavenward. "I will impress on Brother Gabriel that he may accompany you into the world because that is what he wishes, but only to encourage you in God's great purpose for you."

Then, his face stern, Father Abbot put his hands on Percy's head. Percy closed his eyes. "Just as our Lord encountered the good thief at the moment of His crucifixion and forgave him, I charge you, Brother Percy, be the good thief. And if you ever wish it, this monastery will always be your home."

Later, when Father Abbot summoned me and told me of his requirements, I happily agreed.

"I know I can trust that you will remain a good and faithful monk, Brother Gabriel, and that you will be a constant source of guidance for Percy's troubled soul, which is not as it should be, you know. The one reason that I am allowing you to go is to lend our support to his salvation."

"I will do my best," I promised, knowing full well how difficult that would be.

The next morning, after Prime, we found Adrien Sax and three horses waiting in the forecourt. All the brother monks had turned out to bid us farewell, with hugs, tears, prayers, and a few kisses. Finally, we mounted and reined our horses toward the stone bridge, and as I looked back to the gates and the monks waving their good-byes, I wondered if I would ever again see the only home I had ever known.

Plan of the Monastery
of St. Ambrose

1- Church & Chapel
2- Cloister
3- Refectory
4- Guest House
5- Crypt of St. Hilda

6- Dorter
7- Nightstairs
8- Locutory
9- Scholarium
10- Warming Room

11- Tower
12- Brew House
13- Bake House
14- Gate
15- Forecourt

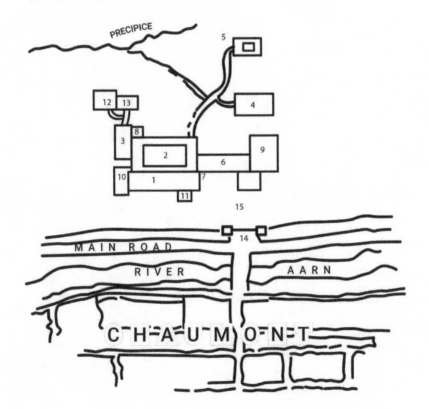

Glossary

Ahriman. The Zoroastrian religion of ancient Persia (about 600 BC). It recognized two dominant deities in the universe. The more powerful of the two was *Ahura Mazda*, the Spirit of Good. *Ahriman* was the Spirit of Evil. Humans, the Persians believed, were free to follow either and to choose the path of virtue or sin. Some scholars believe that *Ahriman* was the prototype of Satan, who appears later in the Hebrew, Christian and Islamic traditions.

Ambrose. Saint Ambrose was Bishop of Milan, in the fourth century. He is remembered in Christian history as a great scholar and for his simple lifestyle and piety. He died in 397 AD.

Caroline (or Carolingian) Minuscule. This was a script or font, that was begun around 700 AD and was in full use in Europe between 800 and 1200. It is characterized by clear, rounded letters, spaces between words, and use of some punctuation. It was intended as a clear, uniform Latin script that all literate people could read.

"Chanted" Prayers. In the early Christian Church, even from late-Roman times, there was a strong tradition of chanting prayers. By Gabriel's day, such chanting was done only in monasteries, and the style of chant was known as Gregorian Chant. You can hear an example of it here: https://www.youtube.com/watch?v=W-hrBhA 4XkM

Chorus of Evil Voices. If you wish to listen to what Gabriel is hearing, find *Carmina Burana,* by Carl Orff. https://www.youtube.com/ watch?v=4QPU1VpPn2s&list=RDQEllLECo4OM&index=2

Cloister. Usually a covered or partly-covered area of a monastery's inner pre-cincts, where monks can pray outdoors, usually while walking around a rectangular pathway.

Day of Ashes (Also known as Ash Wednesday). Always forty days before Easter Sunday in the Christian spiritual calendar, it signals the beginning of the Season of Lent — a period of reflection and self-denial. Christians mark the day by putting ashes on their foreheads as a sign of sorrow for sin and a symbol that we all must die one day.

Deuxième Bureau. The French Military Intelligence Agency in the era before the First World War. It mainly gathered foreign intelligence about the mil-itary threat to France represented by Germany and its allies.

Special Branch. (British) A department of Scotland Yard that dealt with mat-ters of espionage.

Tatzelwurm. A lizard-like, cat-faced alpine folk creature. It was said to be ven-omous, and that its putrid breath could overcome humans with headaches and dizziness. Some believe the creatures — reportedly more than seven feet long — to be phantoms of a monster that had inhabited the Alps in earlier times. The creatures are said to invariably announce their presence by emitting a high-pitched hiss.

Trial by Cross. In pre-Christian Germany, the custom was to settle disputes by Ordeals or Trials, in which the person who prevailed as adjudged to be in the right. As the custom continued into Christian times, the person who prevailed was considered to be declared in the right by God. Trial by Com-bat was the usual form of Ordeal, but Emperor Charlemagne considered it unseemly for churchmen to settle disputes by combat, so he invented

Trial by Cross. The trial represented, in part, the agonies that Jesus must have felt on the cross.

Triple Entente. An Alliance between England, France, and Russia, negotiated in 1907, and generally intended to oppose German ambitions in Europe.

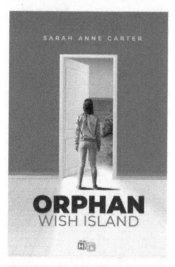